This girl didn't lo... had a round, merry face and bright, blue, inquisitive eyes that peered out through a fringe of sandy-coloured hair. The fringe was rather long and straggly, while the rest of the hair was chopped off short, with her ears poking through it on either side like a pixie's. She looked funny, but nice.

As she reached Elizabeth, she said: 'Hallo!' Gravely, Elizabeth said: 'Hallo.' They stood looking at each other.

'What's your name?'

'Elizabeth Muir,' said Elizabeth.

'I'm Paddy Dewar.'

YOU TWO

Jean Ure

Illustrated by Martin White

Beaver Books

A Beaver Book

Published by Arrow Books Limited
17–21 Conway Street, London W1P 6JD

An imprint of the Hutchinson Publishing Group

London Melbourne Sydney Auckland
Johannesburg and agencies throughout the world

First published by Hutchinson 1984
Beaver edition 1985

Text © Jean Ure 1984
Illustrations © Martin White 1984

Set in Linoterm Baskerville

Made and printed in Great Britain
by Anchor Brendon Ltd
Tiptree, Essex

ISBN 0 09 938310 1

1

Elizabeth had known for a long time that things were changing. She could even pinpoint the very day on which they had started to do so – a Monday morning about six months ago, when her father hadn't gone to work; instead of rolling his umbrella and picking up his brief case and setting off for the station at precisely ten minutes past eight, which was what he had been doing every weekday morning for as long as she could remember, he had simply poured himself a second cup of coffee and settled back in his chair with his newspaper spread upon his knee and shown every sign of staying there.

Such a thing had never happened before. Timmy, busy ransacking the cereal packet in search of plastic dinosaurs, had wanted to know 'whether it was holidays?' Elizabeth could have told him that it wasn't. How could it be, when they were still in the middle of term? Mr Muir only had holidays when everyone else did. But in that case, what was he doing, sitting over breakfast when he ought to be out catching his train?

He couldn't be ill, because if he was ill he would be in bed; and anyway, he didn't look ill. He looked just the same as he always did – except that it was a Monday morning and he was still wearing his week-end sweater and his old grey trousers. He never went to the office in his weekend sweater and old trousers. His office clothes were quite different. They were suits and ties and crackly shirts. Elizabeth had been just as puzzled as Timmy. She'd known it wasn't holidays, but she couldn't think of any other explanation.

It had been their mother who had told them: 'Daddy's firm has had to close down. It didn't have enough money to pay people with, so it's gone into what's known as voluntary liquidation.' (Elizabeth had had visions of lots of men in suits and ties and crackly shirts squeezing themselves into a giant liquidizer and coming out at the other end all pulped, like oranges.) 'That means that Daddy won't be going there any more. He's got to find another firm to work for.'

Term had ended, and summer holidays had come and gone. Elizabeth had grown quite used to being the only member of the family who had to leave home after breakfast every morning. She had grown used to seeing her father there when she came back for lunch at twelve o'clock and still there when she came back again for tea at four. At first it hadn't seemed right. She'd even felt a bit hard done by, a bit excluded, having to go off by herself every day while they all stayed at home, doing things without her; but then the new term had begun, and Timmy had started at his nursery school, which meant that he wasn't there either, and after that it hadn't seemed so bad. In fact, it had *almost* come to seem natural.

They were one week into the winter term by now, and Mr Muir had found himself another firm that had enough money to pay people with, though Elizabeth knew, from the way he and her mother talked about it when they thought she wasn't listening – 'We'll have to economize, of course,' and, 'It'll mean making fairly drastic cuts' – that it didn't have as much money as the other firm had had before it had put itself into the liquidizer. The little red Mini that her mother used for shopping, and sometimes for running Elizabeth to school in when the weather was bad, disappeared from the garage, and Mr Muir's big blue Armstrong Siddeley was taken away and a modest Ford Cortina came to take its place. Elizabeth actually preferred the Cortina, because it was all new and shiny from the show-room, whereas the Armstrong Siddeley had been old and smelt of leather, but when she said as much to her father, venturing to suggest that 'a new car *must* be better than an old one, mustn't it?' he only pulled a face and said: 'Needs must when the devil drives . . . I cannot pretend to be enchanted.'

The new firm that he was working for was further away than the other one had been. Now he left home every morning before Elizabeth was even dressed, and sometimes didn't arrive back until Timmy had had his bath and been put to bed. A big 'FOR SALE' notice appeared in the front garden, and envelopes from estate agents began dropping through the letter box with every post, containing details of 'architect-designed town houses with spacious dining areas and underfloor central heating' and '1930s' brick-built semis with all mod. cons close to schools and shops'. It was really no surprise when one day at tea time her mother said: 'Well! I've got a piece of news for you two . . . how would you like to move to a new house?'

Timmy, his mouth agape over more bread and butter than it could comfortably accommodate, turned with big eyes to Elizabeth, seeking guidance. *Would* they like to move to a new house?

Elizabeth, whose nature was cautious, said *'Really* new?'

'Really really new . . . as new as new can be . . . we'll be the very first people ever to have lived there. It's not quite as big as Deepdene (Deepdene was the name of their present house) so we'll have to have a bit of a clear-out, see what toys you can both bear to part with – there's that old tricycle of yours, for instance, Timmy. I'm sure that could go – and all those dolls of Elizabeth's. You never seem to play with them. We could give them to the PDSA and help the animals. You wouldn't mind doing that, would you?'

'I suppose not,' said Elizabeth. And then, stricken with sudden doubts: 'There will be room for William, won't there?' William was the family cat. He was large and ginger and looked like a tea cosy. Just at the moment he was sitting purring on the table at Elizabeth's elbow, waiting for his share of bread and butter. 'We won't be leaving *him* behind?'

'Good gracious me, no! The very idea! Leave William? Your father wouldn't hear of it!'

Elizabeth relaxed.

'That's all right, then. You can give the dolls away – and the doll's house as well, if you like. *And* those puppet things. I don't want those any more.'

'Let's wait and see. We don't have to go mad

and throw out everything . . . the place isn't as small as all that!'

She didn't care how small it was so long as William was going with them. It could be a hut for all she cared. She held him out a corner of bread and butter.

'I hope it's near his friends.' William had two friends: one was a tabby cat called Jasmine, and the other was a Siamese called Samantha. Both of them fawned on him and brought him presents of dead mice. 'He wouldn't be happy,' said Elizabeth, 'if he couldn't see them every day.'

'Oh, don't you worry . . . he'll soon find himself more foolish females to pander to him.'

'You mean it *isn't* near?'

'No, we're going to leave Caterham altogether. We're going to move into Croydon, instead.'

'Oh.' That *had* been a surprise: it had never occurred to her that they might be leaving Caterham. Caterham was where she had been born – where she had lived, all her life. She looked at her mother, bewildered. 'What are we doing that for?' she said.

'Well, it will make it easier for Daddy's job, for one thing. It will cut down the amount of travelling. He'll be able to leave later in the morning and get back earlier at night. Of course, it's going to mean that you'll have to go to a different school—' That was another surprise. Elizabeth set down her bread and butter and stared. '—but I don't expect you'll mind that. You'll soon make lots of new friends, just as William will – just as we all will. It's going to be quite an adventure for everybody.'

There was a pause. Then in a small, incredulous voice, Elizabeth said: 'You mean, I've got to leave Lady Margaret?'

'I'm afraid there simply isn't any alternative. You can't come in all the way from Croydon every day.'

'Some people do. Some people come by train. There's a girl called Christine Cottle who does.'

'She's probably older than you.'

'She isn't, she's in the same form.'

'Well, then, obviously her parents don't mind. I wouldn't be happy for you to travel all that way every day. It's far too much. There's a fifteen minute walk to the station before you even start.'

'I can walk fifteen minutes!'

'Yes, I know you can, but I still wouldn't be happy. In any case, it isn't just the travelling. Daddy and I have already discussed it together, and we're both agreed that it's probably all for the best if you *do* have a change. Lady Margaret has been excellent in its way, but you're growing up now; you can't always be sheltered. It's about time you went to a – well, to a proper school. The sort of school that everyone else has to go to. It's a pity it's in the middle of term, but that unfortunately can't be helped. Anyway, you'll soon settle down. Gladeside isn't one of the really enormous comprehensives – I wouldn't let you go to one of those. It's bigger than Lady Margaret, of course—'

'How much bigger?' said Elizabeth.

'Oh! Quite a lot. Lady Margaret is tiny. That's one of the reasons why we sent you there in the first place, we thought you'd do better – and you have, you've done very well and we're very pleased

10

with you, but there are certain things that Lady Margaret can't offer—'

'What things?'

'Well, learning how to mix with people. Different people. At Gladeside you'll meet all sorts – boys as well as girls. And then they've got their own swimming pool and their own playing fields, which you'll like – and no school uniform. You'll be able to wear whatever you want. Just think of that!'

Elizabeth thought of it, and wrinkled her nose. She liked her school uniform. At Lady Margaret it was very distinctive: brown blazers with gold braid, and badges in the shape of a shield, with a Latin motto which said 'Ora et Labora' (which meant 'Pray and Work') and berets, quartered in brown and gold, instead of ordinary hats, and ties in brown and gold stripes, and cream blouses and brown pleated skirts, so that when you walked down the High Street everyone knew that you were a Lady Margaret girl and it made you feel as if you were someone special. School wouldn't seem like school without a uniform. She said as much to her mother, but Mrs Muir only laughed and said: 'My goodness me, aren't you regimented! Next thing you'll be telling me you'd rather be known by a number than a name!'

'We are,' said Elizabeth, 'when we take exams.'

'Yes, and that's another thing . . . at Gladeside you'll be able to have a choice – GCE or CSE. *And* there's a proper sixth form. If you stayed on at Lady Margaret, you'd have to transfer at sixteen. You wouldn't be very happy about that.'

Sixteen was still five whole years off. What was

the point of worrying about sixteen? It was *now* that mattered.

Trying rather too obviously to make things seem better, her mother said: 'Timmy will have to go to a new school as well, you know, and it's worse for him. He's only just started. You'll take it in your stride. Think of the advantages you'll have! You're bound to be way ahead of everyone. Not that that will mean you're necessarily any cleverer, but it will mean that you can more than hold your own.' Her mother looked at her, hopefully. 'That should make you feel good, shouldn't it?'

'Will they play netball?' said Elizabeth. She wouldn't mind so much if they played netball. Netball was something they couldn't do at Lady Margaret because of not having any netball court. All they did was tennis twice a week in the local park, and games with bean bags in the gym.

'Oh, I should think so!' said her mother. 'With their own playing fields, I should think they play everything. They probably have a Sports Day, as well. You'll be able to run races and do jumping, and all sorts of things . . . I'm sure it won't be anywhere *near* as bad as you think.'

Elizabeth's best friend at Lady Margaret (which in full was Lady Margaret Foster's College for Girls) was called Jenny Bell. She was very small and plump and pretty, with fair hair that curled, whereas Elizabeth was quite tall for her age, rather on the thin side, ordinary-looking without being plain, and with hair that was dark and straight and on weekdays had to be done in old-fashioned pigtails because of a school rule about long hair

13

not being worn loose. She and Jenny had been best friends for almost two years, so that when Elizabeth, at break next morning in the tiny playground, said, 'I'm not going to be coming here much longer,' she did expect Jenny to show *some* concern. She was sure she would have shown concern if it had been Jenny who was leaving. Instead, hardly pausing in her usual break-time task of dividing a tube of Smarties into seven different rows, according to their colours, Jenny said only: 'Can't your parents afford the fees any more?'

'Of course they can,' said Elizabeth.

'So why won't you be coming here?'

'Because we're moving.'

'That's what Karin Ellis is doing.' Calmly, Jenny picked up three odd Smarties which were ruining her pattern and put them into her mouth. 'She's leaving at the end of term.'

'I've got to leave before that,' said Elizabeth. 'I've got to leave in only a few weeks.'

'You'll miss Speech Day,' said Jenny. She removed four red Smarties from the bottom row. 'Karin Ellis's parents are going to Canada.'

'We're going to Croydon,' said Elizabeth.

'*Croydon?*' Jenny sat back on her heels on the grass. 'We go into Croydon every Saturday.'

'So do we,' said Elizabeth. 'Sometimes,' she added.

'Well, *Croydon* isn't very far. Christine Cottle lives in Croydon.'

'Yes, I know.'

'She comes in by train. She has a season ticket.'

'Yes,' said Elizabeth. 'I know.'

14

'So why can't you do that? Then you wouldn't have to leave.'

'Yes,' said Elizabeth, 'I *know*. I already asked them. They won't let me.'

'Why not?'

'They just won't.'

'I bet it's because they can't afford it.'

'It's not because they can't afford it.'

'I bet it is. My mother says with the price of everything going up it's a wonder that anyone can.'

'My parents can. If they wanted to. It's because they don't want to. They'd rather I started going to a proper school.'

'This *is* a proper school.'

'Not like the one I'm going to.'

'Why?' Jenny looked at her, jealously. 'What's so proper about the one you're going to?'

Elizabeth searched her memory: just for a moment, she couldn't think. Then she did.

'It's got its own playing fields,' she said. '*And* its own swimming pool.'

'So what?'

'Well, it's bigger – and it has boys.'

'Ugh! It sounds horrible.'

'No, it doesn't.'

'Yes, it does. It sounds *horrible*.'

'Why does it sound horrible?'

'Having *boys*.' Jenny scooped up the last of her Smarties and crammed them into her mouth. 'I bet you *hate* it,' she said.

Later that morning, Miss Hutton, who was their form mistress, called Elizabeth up to her desk as the others were leaving and said: 'I'm sure you can't wait to kick the dust from your heels, but just because you're going to a new school it's not very nice, is it, do you think, to start running down the old one?'

Elizabeth felt her cheeks grow pink.

'I wasn't,' she said.

'Weren't you?' Miss Hutton looked at her, steadily. 'You haven't been boasting about going to somewhere bigger and better? Somewhere with its own playing fields and its own swimming pool?'

Elizabeth said nothing.

'I don't deny,' said Miss Hutton, 'that it must be very *nice* to have one's own playing fields, and one's own private swimming pool, but there are other things in life, you know, Elizabeth.'

Of course she knew. She said desperately: 'I wasn't boasting. *Honestly*. I was just saying.'

'Well! Perhaps, in the circumstances, it wasn't very tactful?' Miss Hutton's stern expression relaxed slightly. 'It did rather make it sound as if you couldn't be bothered with us any more, and I don't think that that is the case, is it?'

'*No!*' said Elizabeth.

'I thought it couldn't be. So, tell me . . . which school are you going to?'

'Gladeside High,' said Elizabeth.

'Gladeside?' Miss Hutton paused, in her stacking of exercise books. She seemed a little surprised. 'Well! I hope you'll like it there. You'll have to be prepared to adapt, you know. You'll find it very different from Lady Margaret.'

'Yes, I know,' said Elizabeth.

She said that she knew, but really and truly she

didn't. She couldn't imagine a school that was any different from Lady Margaret.

'I shall be interested to hear how you get on,' said Miss Hutton. She gathered up her exercise books and stowed them away in her brief case. 'You'll have to write and tell us all about it, then if the letter is good enough I can pin it on the notice board. And if it's *really* good—' she smiled, as Elizabeth held open the door '—I *might* even put it in the school magazine . . .'

2

Elizabeth had expected Gladeside High to be different from Lady Margaret, because everyone had told her that it would be; but not all the telling in the world could have prepared her for the shock of just *how* different. The first thing that was different was the actual building. Lady Margaret had been two old houses knocked into one, with a circular drive in front and a walled garden behind. Not even an infant could have got lost in Lady Margaret. Gladeside, by contrast, seemed almost as large as a town. The buildings were purpose built, all shining glass and flashing metal, with vast flights of stone steps and broad, straight corridors that went on for ever.

When Elizabeth and her mother arrived, dragging Timmy by the hand because there hadn't been anyone to leave him with, the corridors were empty: morning assembly was already over, and all the pupils safely locked away behind closed doors. They went into an office where a lady sitting at a desk was opening letters with a letter opener in the shape of a dagger. She looked up at them and smiled and said: 'You'll be Mrs Muir and Elizabeth. I'll take you straight in to the Head Master. He is expecting you.'

That was another difference: *Head Master*. At

Lady Margaret they had had Miss Lowman; at Gladeside they had Mr Farmer. Miss Lowman had been tall and elegant, with dark hair pulled back into a bun and gold-rimmed spectacles that hung about her neck on a chain. She had worn well-cut suits of charcoal grey or navy blue, and had smelt very faintly of flowers. Mr Farmer was neither tall nor elegant, and he certainly didn't smell of flowers. He was short, and rather stumpy, with red hair that stuck up in tufts and a green tweed suit that was all baggy at the knees and had a decided aroma of pipe. (Which was, in its way, quite comforting, since it reminded Elizabeth of Grandpa Muir, who was never seen without clouds of smoke billowing about his head.)

Mr Farmer said: 'Well, Elizabeth! I hope you'll quickly learn to settle down and be happy with us. If you have any problems, you can always bring them to me. That's what I'm here for: I'm not just a figurehead. Never be afraid to approach me. Now, then, let me see . . .' He pulled a sheet of paper towards him and ran a finger down a long list of names. 'Yes. I've put you in Class 1C.'

1C? She stared at him, her face crimson. C was for dunces. At Lady Margaret, they had always separated every year into three different groups, A for the clever ones, B for the not so clever, and C for the ones that weren't clever at all. Right from the very start, Elizabeth had always been in the A group.

Mr Farmer smiled, reassuringly, and shook his head.

'Oh, you needn't worry! The C doesn't mean anything – we don't have streaming here. It's just a useful way of dividing people up.'

She didn't think she liked that. It might be just a useful way of dividing people up, but how could she tell them at Lady Margaret that she was in *1C?* And how could you ever be expected to learn anything if you were all mixed up together, bright ones and not so bright ones and those that were just plain stupid? She shot her mother a worried glance, but Mrs Muir was already standing up, preparing to take her leave. Elizabeth felt a moment of panic. She pictured her mother walking back down the road, with Timmy bobbing up and down at her side, chattering away in his silly little high-pitched squeak, not caring that she had been left here all by herself, among strangers. She pictured them doing the shopping together – going back home together – talking to William, eating jam doughnuts – not *caring*. She wanted to scream, 'Please don't leave me here! Let me come with you! Please!' but of course she didn't. Mrs Muir said: 'We'll see you at lunch time, then. All right?' and she heard her own voice, in reply: 'Yes. All right.' It sounded a little wobbly, but at least it didn't break.

After her mother and Timmy had gone, Mr Farmer introduced her to the lady in the outer office, who now sat typing.

'Elizabeth, this is my secretary, Miss George. If ever you want to see me, you must come to Miss George first, and she will make an appointment. Never be afraid of asking – I'll be back in one moment, Miss George. I'm just taking Elizabeth along to her classroom.'

He led her out of the office, down one of the long corridors until they came to a flight of steps, up the flight of steps and down another corridor, along a covered walkway with windows that looked out on to a playground where girls in shorts were playing netball, down another corridor, up some more steps – Elizabeth very soon gave up trying to memorize the route. She knew that it was hopeless: she would never be able to find her way back. Even if she did want to see Miss George to make an appointment, she wouldn't be able to.

'It's not nearly as complicated as it seems,' said Mr Farmer. 'You'll soon get it sorted out . . . here we are! This is 1C.'

That was the next shock: 1C looked almost as large as the whole of Lady Margaret put together. She afterwards discovered that there were only thirty-nine of them (Elizabeth herself brought the number up to forty) but even thirty-nine was bad enough when you were used to no more than sixteen. It might not have seemed quite so many if they had been ranged tidily and were wearing uniform, but instead of neat brown skirts and cream blouses they were all wearing just whatever they chose – greens, and reds, and purples, even *jewellery* – and instead of sitting up straight at their desks as they had been taught to do at Lady Margaret they were all slumped anyhow, some with their legs stuck out into the gangway, some with their heads resting on their hands, some with their arms folded, some leaning back in their chairs – Miss Hutton would have been horrified. She would have lectured them on manners and handed out order marks all round.

Mr Farmer didn't say a word. He didn't seem to care how his pupils sat, or how they dressed. He didn't even seem to care that no one stood up when he came in. He simply put a hand on Elizabeth's shoulder, and firmly propelling her towards the front of the room said: 'Mrs Hyslop, good morning to you! This is Elizabeth Muir. You'll remember I did speak to you about her. Mrs Hyslop is your class teacher, Elizabeth. She'll tell you where to sit and what books you need. I'll leave you in her care.'

The next minute and he, too, was gone. The last link with her mother had disappeared, and now she was truly on her own. Elizabeth, by herself, and 1C. And, of course, Mrs Hyslop. Mrs Hyslop was youngish, and quite pleasant-looking, but seemed too preoccupied with what she was doing, which was adding up columns of figures in some kind of a register, to have any time to spare for a new pupil. She handed Elizabeth a blank sheet of paper, marked off into sections, and told her to 'Go and sit over there, next to Jo Ann. She'll show you how to make up your timetable, and where to go when you have a change of classroom.'

Jo Ann was a black girl. There hadn't been any black girls at Lady Margaret – not black like Jo Ann was. There'd been an Indian girl called Devi, and a girl who'd been born in Malta, but they'd been more brown, or cocoa-coloured. Jo Ann was definitely black. She had frizzy black hair which she had plaited into two tight pigtails which stuck out on either side of her head. Elizabeth knew she mustn't stare, because staring at people who were different from yourself was rude, even if you were only doing it out of natural curiosity, so she smiled, instead, and said hallo. Jo Ann didn't return the smile. She only looked at Elizabeth rather sullenly and mumbled something that might or might not have been 'hallo' in return. Perhaps, thought

Elizabeth, she resented having a new girl being sent to sit next to her, though since hers was the only desk with a vacant seat it was difficult to know where else she could have gone. She was thankful, at any rate, that the desk wasn't one of the ones on the central gangway. On the other side of the gangway was where the boys sat, and although originally she had thought it might be fun to be in the same form with boys, now that she had actually seen them she wasn't so sure. She had never known any boys apart from Timmy, who was too young to count, and Jenny Bell's brother, Stephen, who went to a school called Winchcombe House, where all the masters wore black cloaks and funny flat hats with tassels which Jenny said were mortar boards. Stephen always looked very pink and scrubbed. The boys in 1C didn't look either pink *or* scrubbed. They looked rough, and alien, like the boys who served you in the market on a Saturday morning. At least where she was sitting with Jo Ann she couldn't be seen by them.

'Here.' She found a sheet of paper being thrust under her nose. 'You better copy this. You got a pen?'

'Yes, thank you,' said Elizabeth. She had her special new fountain pen, which had been given to her on her birthday, because at Lady Margaret you weren't allowed to use ball points or felt tips. Miss Hutton said it spelt death to handwriting. Neatly, watched by Jo Ann, she began filling in the empty boxes on her timetable. *English: Mrs Hyslop. Civics: Mrs Hyslop*—

'What you gonna do,' said Jo Ann, 'when that thing run out?'

'It's got a cartridge,' said Elizabeth. She stopped writing and unscrewed the top of the pen to show her. 'You just put another refill in. It's like a ball point, except it's real ink.'

'What you wanna bother using real ink for?'

'It isn't any bother, it's easy as pie. Anyway, it's better for your handwriting. Ball points spoil it.'

Jo Ann didn't say anything to this; only put a finger in her mouth and began chewing at her fingernail. Elizabeth screwed the top back on her pen. Miss Hutton hadn't let people chew finger-nails. Chewing fingernails was supposed to be bad for you. She went on with her copying. *French: Mr Boyden. Arithmetic: Miss Slade. Cookery: Mrs Hepple. Geography: Mr Ward—*

'When do we have Latin?' she said.

Jo Ann spoke without removing her finger from her mouth.

'Don't do Latin.'

'Don't do Latin?' said Elizabeth. She had thought everybody did Latin, the same as they did English and arithmetic. 'Not *ever*?'

Jo Ann shrugged a shoulder.

'Not far's I know . . . who'd want to learn a language what nobody don't speak no more? Waste of time, innit?'

Elizabeth was silent. Miss Hutton hadn't seemed to think it was a waste of time, when she'd started teaching them at the beginning of that term. Elizabeth hadn't thought it was a waste of time, either. She'd quite enjoyed learning about *'mensa'* being a table and *'agricola'* being a farmer. On the other hand what Jo Ann said was quite right: nobody *did* speak it. It wasn't as if it were a proper

25

language, like French. At least she knew they did French because she had already copied it into the timetable. She had also copied civics and handicrafts and PE, none of which they had done at Lady Margaret. She wasn't even sure what they were. She filled in a double period of PE for Friday afternoon and turned to Jo Ann.

'What *is* PE?' she said. She hoped it was something nice, since they had almost a whole afternoon of it, not to mention other sessions earlier in the week.

Jo Ann took her finger out of her mouth and stared at her as if she were mad. 'It's games,' she said, 'innit?'

'You mean like netball, and hockey, and things?'

'Yeah; sometimes. When it's not raining. When it's raining we got to go into the hall and do races.'

Jo Ann looked as if she would be good at doing races. She had broad shoulders, like a boy's, and long legs, encased, Elizabeth had been amazed to see, in blue jeans. (Imagine being allowed to wear *jeans*. Miss Hutton would have had a fit.)

'You're gonna need books,' said Jo Ann. 'You can get 'em from Julie.' She nodded towards a pretty, flaxen-haired girl sitting a few seats away. 'She's in charge of stationery. She'll give 'em you . . . hey, Julie!' She called across. The flaxen-haired girl looked round. 'She wants some books an' things.' Jo Ann jerked her thumb towards Elizabeth. 'You gonna get her some?'

'S'pose I'll have to.' Julie left her seat and went up to the desk, where Mrs Hyslop was still ticking things off in her register. 'Is it all right if I give the new girl some stationery?'

Mrs Hyslop nodded, without speaking, and handed over a key. With an air of consequence, Julie took it and strutted across to a large cupboard in the corner of the room.

'Here you are.' She dumped a pile of assorted exercise books on Elizabeth's desk. 'There's one for English, one for French, one for geography, one for history, one for arithmetic, one for rough, one for general. If you need any more, you'll have to come to me. I'm the only one that can give them to you because I'm in charge of stationery.'

She bounced off again, self-importantly, to her place. Elizabeth looked down at her stack of exercise books. They weren't nearly as nice as the ones they'd had at Lady Margaret. At Lady Margaret they'd had ones with stiff covers, and special printed labels with the school badge and the letters 'LMFCG' over the top of it. These were all thin and flimsy and didn't have any sort of label at all.

'You got to put your name on the front,' said Jo Ann. 'With the name of the class and the name of the subject.'

Obediently, Elizabeth began doing so. One for English, one for French, one for geography, one for history, one for arithmetic, one for general—

'Don't we have one for prep?' she said.

Jo Ann looked at her, blankly.

'Prep notebook,' said Elizabeth. 'To write down what's for prep.'

There was a pause.

'Dunno what you're talking about,' said Jo Ann.

'*Prep*,' said Elizabeth. 'Don't you do it?' Really, what with no Latin, and no uniform, and now no

27

prep, this seemed a very peculiar sort of school. 'You mean nobody ever gives us any work that we have to do at home?'

'Oh! That. Yeah, some of 'em give it us. Mrs Hyslop, she does.'

Then why couldn't she have said so? wondered Elizabeth, puzzled. Why did she pretend not to know about it?

'So where do we write it down,' she said, 'if we don't have any prep notebooks?'

An expression of faint irritation crossed Jo Ann's face.

'What's all this with prep? What you keep going on about prep for?'

'You just said that you did it. That Mrs Hyslop—' Elizabeth faltered. She could see that she was annoying the other girl, but she couldn't understand how. She'd only wanted to find out where you wrote down what prep you had to do. At Lady Margaret they'd had special blue notebooks for it. Perhaps they didn't have any at Gladeside – perhaps that was why Jo Ann was getting cross with her, because she thought she was criticizing. 'I don't expect it really matters,' she said. 'I expect you could write it anywhere.'

'Write what?' said Jo Ann, dangerously.

'What you have to do when you get home—'

'*Homework,*' said Jo Ann. 'If that's what you mean, why don't you say?'

She didn't quite like, after that, to ask what civics and handicraft were. For the next few minutes she sat in silence, keeping her head bent over her new exercise books, while Jo Ann turned round and carried on a conversation with a girl on the desk

28

behind. It was a relief when at last a bell rang, announcing the beginning of the first period.

English with Mrs Hyslop was reassuringly like English with Miss Rolfe had been at Lady Margaret. Mrs Hyslop handed back essays that she had set last week, and then read out the six best for people to comment upon. The only difference was that at Gladeside essays weren't called essays but compositions, and some of the grammar in the six that were read out was so terrible that Elizabeth couldn't think how Mrs Hyslop had come to let it pass. Miss Rolfe would never have done so. One in particular was so bad that Elizabeth almost laughed, the mistakes were so elementary. If it hadn't been for the mistakes it might have been quite interesting. It was all about a boy who stole things from Woolworth's, and how the police had come for him and taken him to the juvenile court, which wasn't the sort of subject anyone at Lady Margaret would ever have written about (at Lady Margaret it had mostly been holidays and pets and visits to the theatre) but how could you take it seriously when all the verbs were in the wrong person and there quite obviously wasn't any punctuation?

When Mrs Hyslop asked for comments, Elizabeth put up her hand. It was the first time she had dared to do so, but she knew that what she had to say was right.

'I think it's a pity,' she said, 'that he didn't take more care over writing it. I think if he'd bothered a bit more about the grammar it would have been quite good.'

There was a silence. The boy whose composition

29

it was turned slowly to look at her. He was pale, and skinny, with a large nose and thin, mouse-coloured hair. He stared at her, accusingly. Elizabeth was sorry if she had upset him, but after all she had said no more than the truth. It was only what Miss Rolfe would have said. 'I will not have slipshod work.' That was what Miss Rolfe always used to say. 'I will not have slipshod work: slipshod work betokens a slipshod mind.'

'Well, now,' said Mrs Hyslop. 'Shall I tell you what I think, Elizabeth? I think it's a pity if we're so busy looking out for grammatical errors that we fail to see the wood for the trees . . . I'm not saying that grammar isn't important, obviously it is. But what is even more important is having something to say – which I think Sammy's composition does. It may not be perfectly expressed, but it has the ring of truth about it. It comes alive – it holds one's attention. I only wish I had a few more like it.'

Sammy glowed, while Elizabeth felt snubbed. Mrs Hyslop hadn't spoken unkindly, but it was obvious she disagreed with what Elizabeth had said. And yet what she had said had been *right*. She knew that it had, because it was what Miss Rolfe always said. 'Learn the rules first, then you can apply them. There's no point in having brilliant ideas if you don't know how to set them down on paper.' Mrs Hyslop had it all the wrong way round.

She didn't put up her hand any more, in case Mrs Hyslop had other things the wrong way round, as well. She didn't like being snubbed; nobody had ever snubbed her at Lady Margaret. She wished that she was back there.

After English they had civics, which was also

taught by Mrs Hyslop. Elizabeth still didn't know what civics was, but from the things that were talked about she gathered it had something to do with drains and public libraries. It seemed an odd combination, but last week, apparently, 1C had been on a visit to the junior library and had written accounts of it, and now they were learning all about drains so that in a few weeks' time they could go on a visit to a sewage farm and write an account of that. At the mention of the words 'sewage farm' some of the boys began making noises as if they were going to be sick, and a girl in the front row, who had already been cautioned several times for talking, held her nose and said loudly, 'Ugh! Pooh! It'll pong!' Mrs Hyslop told the boys to be quiet and the girl to stop being childish. Elizabeth thought she was being rather unfair. A sewage farm probably *would* pong. She wasn't at all sure that she wanted to visit a sewage farm. She would far rather have gone to the junior library.

When civics was over, it was break, and everyone went crashing and stamping out of the room. Elizabeth stood for a moment, uncertain, then Jo Ann, halfway to the door, jerked her head and said impatiently, 'Come on, then, if you're coming,' and relieved she hurried after her. Her relief was short-lived. After leading her back along the corridor and down a flight of steps, Jo Ann flapped a careless hand said, 'There's the lavs – playground's out there. See ya,' and disappeared.

Elizabeth was left by herself. Boys and girls thronged on either side of her, but nobody stopped to talk, because nobody knew who she was. At Lady Margaret, everyone had known. At Lady Margaret, she had been Elizabeth Muir, who was in Miss Hutton's form and best friends with Jenny Bell and had once won a prize for English. Here she wasn't anybody. The place was too big, it was huge – it was *hateful*. Quite suddenly, she felt as if she was going to cry.

The only thing that stopped her was pride. You didn't cry in public – not at her age. It would be too shameful. Blinking back tears, she walked out into the playground, where almost at once she saw Jo Ann, playing netball with a crowd of other girls. They were running up and down, passing to each other. As Elizabeth stood wistfully watching, someone threw the ball too high, way over Jo Ann's head, so that tall as she was and as high as she jumped she still couldn't reach it. It came rolling and bouncing over the asphalt, towards Elizabeth. This was her chance! Eagerly, she stooped to pick it up, throwing it over-arm, as she had seen the others throw it, back again to Jo Ann.

'Here!'

'Ta.' Jo Ann plucked the ball coolly out of the air with one hand. For just a second she seemed to hesitate, as if on the point of asking Elizabeth whether she would like to join in; then someone shouted, 'Come on, Jo-Jo! Chuck it!' and with a slight grimace, half as if in apology, half as if to say, 'I've got better things to do than worry about stupid new girls,' she turned and went racing back to the game. Elizabeth swallowed. Perhaps tomorrow – tomorrow, they would ask her. In the meantime, she was not going to cry, because crying didn't help and besides it was *shameful*.

Back in the classroom at the end of break, Jo Ann

said: 'Ugh! *French!*' Elizabeth cheered up slightly. She was quite good at French; she had almost come top in it last term. Encouraged, she said: 'Don't you like it?'

'*Stupid* bloody language,' said Jo Ann.

After a second's startled pause, Elizabeth said: 'What book d'you have? D'you have *France Aujourd'hui*? That's the one we had.'

Jo Ann flung the lid of her desk open.

'Ain't got no books yet. Only started this term. Far as I'm concerned—' she slammed the lid down again '—might as well *finish* this term an' all.'

French was taken by Mr Boyden, who was elderly and egglike, with a head that was completely bald except for two long, lank strips which fell down over his ears. Mr Boyden didn't teach French as they had at Lady Margaret, out of a book, with long lists of verbs and nouns that had to be learnt off by heart. In some ways it was more fun, because it was like a sort of game. After asking one or two people at random *'Quelle heure est-il?'* or *'Comment allez-vous?'* (Elizabeth wished that he would ask her, but he didn't) he began going through the alphabet as if they were playing I Spy. *'Montrez-moi quelque chose qui commence avec un A . . . montrez-moi quelque chose qui commence avec un B . . .'*

Sometimes it was quite difficult. Nobody could think of anything with an A until suddenly the fair-haired girl called Julie Christmas, who was in charge of stationery, pointed to one of the boys and said 'Abdul'. B, however, was easy – Elizabeth had been waiting for it. Her hand shot up: *'La bouche!'*

C was easy, too. Her hand shot up again: *'Le crayon!'*

D she couldn't think of (Julie Christmas and another girl, together, chorused 'John *Diamond*'.) But E and F were simple. E was *'les élèves'* and F was *'la fenêtre'*, and G was going to have been *'la gomme'* – she'd already taken her rubber out of her desk in readiness – but Mr Boyden didn't let her get as far as G.

'Something tells me,' he said, 'that we have here a young lady who has pursued her study of the French tongue for rather longer than the rest of us.' Julie Christmas slewed round in her desk and sent Elizabeth a piercing glare. 'Would I be right?' Elizabeth nodded, suddenly shy. Everyone else had turned, like Julie Christmas, to look at her. 'And when did you start it?'

'Three terms ago,' said Elizabeth. It made her feel almost guilty, as if she hadn't any right to have started it three terms ago when everyone else had only started this term.

Mr Boyden raised an eyebrow.

'Might I inquire which school you were at?'

'Lady Margaret Foster's College for Girls,' said Elizabeth.

Julie Christmas curled her lip. One of the boys said, 'Lady Margaret Foster's College for Girls' and people began sniggering.

'Thank you!' Mr Boyden held up a hand. 'I see no cause for mirth. The fact that one of your fellow pupils has made good use of the educational advantages offered her is to be commended rather than sneered at. However—' his tone mellowed, slightly '—I think, for the future – Elizabeth, is it? – I think for the future we must keep you in reserve. A kind of back-up force . . . give the others a fair crack of the whip, and if they fail to come up with anything, then we'll see what you can do. Does that strike you as being just and equitable? Good! So, then, let us continue . . . *montrez-moi, s'il vous plaît, quelque chose qui commence avec un G.*'

Julie Christmas's hand went shooting up.

'*La gomme!*'

'*La gomme. Bon! Montrez-moi, alors . . .*'

After French they had arithmetic, which had never been one of Elizabeth's best subjects. It was true that 1C were only just starting on the sort of fractions that she had already done ages ago at Lady Margaret, but even so lots of hands went up just as fast as hers to supply answers to questions, and once, when one was put directly to her, she even managed to get it wrong. She didn't exactly do it on purpose, but Jo Ann, next to her, was obviously bursting to give the correct information, and really she didn't care *that* much about being clever at arithmetic. It seemed far more important that Jo Ann should like her. Jo Ann, however, at the end of the lesson, only jeered.

'What's the matter? Din't they teach you arithmetic at that posh school of yours?'

'Yes,' said Elizabeth, humbly, 'but I wasn't very good at it.'

'Well, you can't be good at everything, *can* ya?' said Jo Ann.

'I'm not very good at geography, either.' Elizabeth proffered the information, eagerly. 'In fact, I'm absolutely *hopeless* at geography. I only got forty-two per cent last term.'

From somewhere behind her, a boy's voice echoed in shrill mimicry: 'I only got forty-two per cent last term!'

Elizabeth felt her cheeks grow hot and pink. Jo Ann said: 'You shut your big mouth, Redmond.' And then, to Elizabeth: 'You don't wanna take no notice of that ape. C'mon! Let's go for dinner.'

'I don't stay for dinner,' said Elizabeth.

'S'pose it wouldn't be good enough for you?' Julie Christmas, smiling sweetly, had come up and slipped her arm through Jo Ann's. 'S'pose at Lady Margaret *Foster's* you had caviare to eat?'

She and Jo Ann went off together. She heard them chanting, all the way along the corridor: 'At Lady Margaret *Foster's* . . .'

I hate this place, she thought. I *hate* it.

3

'So how did the morning go?' said Mrs Muir.

Elizabeth toyed unenthusiastically with scrambled eggs on toast.

'All right.'

'Only all right? What lessons did you do?'

'Usual sort of things.'

'And did you find you were way ahead of everyone?'

'Not particularly.'

'Well, I don't suppose you were behind!'

Elizabeth scowled down at her plate. It might have been easier, she thought, if she had been behind. At least then they wouldn't hate her. She knew that they hated her. The boy called Sammy English hated her because she'd told the truth about his essay being badly written, and Julie Christmas hated her because she'd answered all those questions in French, and Jo Ann hated her because – she wasn't quite sure why Jo Ann hated her, but she'd made it very obvious that she did.

'Have you made any friends yet?' said her mother.

She shook her head.

'Well, I expect you will soon. I was talking to a lady in the greengrocer's this morning; she said her daughter goes to Gladeside. Sandra Gower. Have you met her? Apparently she's in the same form as you.'

'Class,' said Elizabeth. 'They don't call them forms.' Like they didn't call prep 'prep', but homework, and the mistresses weren't 'mistresses' but teachers. She'd learnt that people stared at you if you used the wrong expression, so now she was being very careful what she said. 'Forms are things you sit on.'

'Or things that hares sleep in . . . Mrs Gower's asked me round for coffee on Friday morning. They only live five minutes away – Greencourt Avenue. Just round the back. It would be nice for you to have a friend who lived close, you could see each other at weekends. Why don't you find out which one Sandra Gower is, and ask her if you could walk home together? She'd probably be glad of the company. Mrs Gower says she hasn't got many friends at school. Why don't you do that?'

'All right,' said Elizabeth. She wouldn't, of course. It was a horrific idea. 'Please, my mother says I've got to ask you if we can walk home together,' as if they were about five years old. It was just that it was easier to say 'all right' than try to explain why she couldn't possibly.

'Do it this afternoon; as soon as you get back to school. It'll make you feel better if you know somebody.'

When the time came for Elizabeth to leave, her mother and Timmy walked out to the gate to see her off. Timmy was carrying William, clutched awkwardly in his pudgy little-boy arms. He held him up for Elizabeth to kiss goodbye. She bent, and buried her face in his fur as if she was never going to see him again.

'Don't forget,' said her mother, 'find out who Sandra Gower is – and when you come home at tea time there might just be a surprise for you . . . I might just have found the time to whip up a few chocolate pyramids!'

Elizabeth tried to smile, but was too busy fighting back tears. Of what comfort were chocolate pyramids when you still had a whole long afternoon looming before you? It was even worse than it had been this morning: she hadn't known then that everyone was going to hate her.

In spite of walking as slowly as she could, she still arrived back at school a good ten minutes before the bell rang. The playground was full of boys playing football and girls throwing netballs. Mostly they kept to their separate ends, but in the middle was a mixed group of about a dozen who seemed to be engaged in some kind of vast battle. She could see Jo Ann, fighting away in the middle of them. Their shrieks and yells, girls squealing, boys shouting, echoed about the playground, making it sound like a swimming pool.

As Elizabeth stood awkwardly watching, on the sidelines, a girl suddenly detached herself from the group and began trotting towards her. Elizabeth recognized her as the girl who had been told off for talking and for holding her nose and saying 'Pooh!' in Mrs Hyslop's civics class. She wondered, for a moment, whether it could possibly be Sandra Gower, coming across to speak to her. She certainly *looked* as if she were coming to speak to her, but somehow she didn't think that Sandra Gower would be the sort of girl to be told off for talking or to say 'Pooh!' in a civics class. Sandra Gower would be quiet and well-behaved, and would look ordinary and dim. This girl didn't look a bit ordinary or dim. She had a round, merry face and bright blue, inquisitive eyes that peered out through a fringe of sandy-coloured hair. The fringe was rather long and straggly, while the rest of the hair was chopped off short, with her ears poking through it on either side like a pixie's. She looked funny, but nice.

As she reached Elizabeth, she said: 'Hallo!' Gravely, Elizabeth said: 'Hallo.' They stood looking at each other.

'What's your name?'

'Elizabeth Muir,' said Elizabeth.

'I'm Paddy Dewar. Why have you started in the middle of a term?'

'We moved,' said Elizabeth.

'Where from?'

'From Caterham,' said Elizabeth.

There was a pause.

'Are you glad you've come here?'

Elizabeth struggled a moment. She was a truthful girl; she didn't like telling lies. She made a small, non-committal noise in the back of her throat. Paddy looked at her, sympathetically.

'Didn't you want to?'

She humped a shoulder.

'Didn't mind.' That, at least, was true. She *hadn't* minded originally. That was because she hadn't known how horrid it was going to be.

'Don't you think you're going to like it?' said Paddy.

Again, she struggled.

'Not sure.'

'Did you like your old school? Was it better than this one?

'It was different,' said Elizabeth. She knew that she had to be tactful. After all, Paddy couldn't help it if Gladeside was horrid.

Paddy said: 'Different *how*?'

'Well, it was – it was smaller.'

'Was it posh? Did it have a uniform? What colour was it?'

'Brown,' said Elizabeth. 'And gold.'

Thinking of all the Lady Margaret pupils, in their brown and their gold, made her feel even more miserable than she had before. She imagined Miss Hutton walking in to take the afternoon register. She saw them all sitting there – Jenny, and Christine Cottle, and Devi Shah, with the empty desk that up until last week had been hers. Then behind them Sarah Jacobs, and Maxine Rochmann, and—

'I bet you wish,' said Paddy, 'that you were still there.'

Elizabeth didn't say anything. It would have been rude to say yes, but she certainly wasn't going to say no. Paddy considered her a while, in thoughtful fashion, through her fringe.

'I s'pose someone's already asked you to be part of their gang?'

Slowly, Elizabeth shook her head.

'Would you want to be, if they did?'

'Don't know,' said Elizabeth. They hadn't had gangs at Lady Margaret. She'd thought only rough people belonged to them – yobs with flick knives and ugly hair cuts.

'You don't *have* to be,' said Paddy. She pushed her

41

fringe out of her eyes. 'We could be a you-two, if you wanted.'

'What's a you-two?' said Elizabeth.

'It's where two people are best friends and go around together and do things together and everyone says, "Hey, you two." It's better than being in a gang. Anyone can be in a gang. D'you want to?'

A warm glow suffused Elizabeth's heart.

'All right,' she said.

At Paddy's instigation – 'You have to *show* people' – they marched round the playground, arms linked, chanting as they went: 'We're in a you-two, a you-two, a you-two . . .' When they had come full circle and arrived back again on the spot where it had all begun, Paddy said: 'Did you have a best friend at your other school?'

'Yes,' said Elizabeth.

'What was *her* name?'

'Jenny Bell.'

'Was she pretty?'

Elizabeth screwed up her nose, trying to see Jenny as Paddy might have seen her.

'I s'pose so.'

'What colour hair did she have?'

'Fair,' said Elizabeth.

'Fair like Julie's? People think *she's* pretty. I don't. I don't like fair hair. I like dark hair – dark and *straight*. Like yours. Was hers straight?'

'No,' said Elizabeth. 'It was curly.'

'I don't like curly hair. If I had curly hair I'd get it all cut off. Will you go on seeing her, now that you're not at the same school?'

Elizabeth wondered whether she would. There hadn't been any mention of it when they'd said

goodbye. Jenny had just said, 'Hope you like it, where you're going,' and Elizabeth had said, 'I'll write and tell you about it,' but neither of them had said anything about seeing each other.

'I don't expect we will,' she said. 'Not now.'

Paddy seemed pleased at this.

'*Anyway*,' she said, 'she doesn't rhyme like we do ... Elizabeth *Muir* and Paddy *Dewar* ...' She linked her arm through Elizabeth's. 'Where d'you live? D'you live near school?'

'Court Park Gardens,' said Elizabeth.

'Can I come and have tea with you?'

She didn't see why Paddy shouldn't come and have tea with her. Jenny had come lots of times. Of course, Jenny had never actually *invited* herself; she had always waited to be asked. But still, if people were going to be best friends—

'If you invite *me*,' said Paddy, 'then I'll invite you.'

'All right,' said Elizabeth.

'When can I come? Can I come Saturday?'

Elizabeth was cautious.

'I'll have to ask my mother first.'

'When will you ask her?'

'I'll ask her tonight,' said Elizabeth.

'D'you promise?'

'Yes,' said Elizabeth. 'I promise.'

'You promise you won't forget?'

'I couldn't when I've *promised*.'

'Some people do,' said Paddy. 'I was going to tea with Janet Newman once and when I got round there they'd all gone out and she hadn't told me.'

Elizabeth was appalled.

'That's a *terrible* thing to do. I wouldn't *ever* do a thing like that.'

44

'Janet Newman does things like that all the time. She said she'd invite me to her birthday party last term, but she never did. Now that we're a you-two, shall I ask Jo Ann if she'll change places with me so that we can sit together?' Jo Ann didn't seem to have any objection to changing places even though Paddy's desk was right at the front; it was also on the central gangway.

'She likes it because it's near the boys. *She* ought to have been a boy. She wanted to play football this term, but they wouldn't let her. They let her do metalwork instead of domestic science, but they wouldn't let her do football. I wouldn't mind doing metalwork, would you? Shall I ask them if we can?'

Elizabeth hesitated. She had been quite looking forward to domestic science – they'd never done any at Lady Margaret. Metalwork sounded a rather odd thing to do.

'I won't ask if you don't want me to,' said Paddy. 'We've got to do things together now that we're a you-two. There wouldn't be any point otherwise. Look, that girl over there—' she pointed to a round, pink-cheeked girl with curly black hair '—that's Janet Newman that was going to invite me to her party. She's best friends with Julie Christmas. That's Julie Christmas, sitting next to her. Thinks she's the cat's whiskers, just because she always comes top in everything. P'raps now that you're here she won't any more. That girl that's next to Jo Ann's called Dawn Forrest. She's a Plymouth Brother.'

'What's a Plymouth Brother?' said Elizabeth.

'Something to do with religion. She was going to ask me to tea once, but her mother wouldn't let her.

She's only allowed to be friends with other Plymouth Brothers.'

'Crumbs,' said Elizabeth. She stared pityingly at Dawn Forrest, sitting with bent head in the front row. She wondered if she was very holy. 'Which one's Sandra Gower?' she said

'Sandra Gower? She's over there.'

Paddy pointed towards a rather plain-looking girl, whom Elizabeth hadn't noticed before. There wasn't a great deal about her that one would notice. She looked exactly as Elizabeth had thought she would look.

'What's *she* like?'

'Soppy. She's always telling people about these elocution lessons she does . . . Michael and *Moses* have very long *noses* – and Greek *dancing*.' Paddy groaned, and rolled her eyes heavenwards. 'She does Greek *dancing*.'

'Oh,' said Elizabeth.

They'd done Greek dancing at Lady Margaret; *and* they'd done Michael and Moses. She supposed it did sound rather soppy when you didn't know what the purpose of it was. Greek dancing was for giving you grace in movement, and Michael and Moses was for lengthening the 'O' sound. At least, that was what Mrs Kenney had told them.

'Why d'you want to know?' Paddy sounded suddenly suspicious. 'You don't *know* her?'

'No,' said Elizabeth, hastily. She felt, instinctively, that it wouldn't be a good thing to know someone who did Greek dancing and took elocution lessons. And anyway, it was quite true, she didn't know her. She couldn't help it if her mother met people in greengrocer's shops. 'Who's the girl next to her?' she

46

said. The girl next to her was large and lumpish-looking, with a huge, pale face and thick spectacles.

'That's Fat Spencer – that's what Julie calls her. Her name's Pat, so she calls her Fat, because she is. The reason she's fat is she keeps eating things. Rubbers, and that sort of thing.'

'*Rubbers?*' said Elizabeth, startled.

'She does it to show off. She can't help it, she does it all the time. Once she drank a whole bottle of ink. And one time she ate a *candle*. She's absolutely mad. You see that boy that's just come in? That's Redmond. He's been caned more times than any other boy in the whole school. The one with him's Sammy English. He's the one that did that composition. The one you didn't like.'

'It wasn't that I didn't *like* it,' said Elizabeth. 'It was just—'

'And that's John Diamond,' said Paddy. 'The one Redmond's talking to. He's the handsomest boy in all the class. Don't you think so?'

Elizabeth, thus appealed to, began to blush. She couldn't have said whether John Diamond was handsome or not: it embarrassed her too much to look.

'Whenever we have team games,' said Paddy, 'and I have to pick up, I always pick John Diamond first. But as you're my best friend, I promise in future I'll always pick you second.'

'Thank you,' said Elizabeth, genuinely grateful.

During the afternoon break, she and Paddy went round arm in arm again, performing their chant ('We're in a you-two, a you-two, a you-two . . .') and at the end of school it wasn't Sandra Gower she walked home with but Paddy, who insisted on accompanying her even though it added miles to her own journey. Elizabeth was worried, but Paddy said that was the sort of thing you did when you were best friends and that tomorrow morning they could arrange to meet halfway and go in together.

'But only if you really want to.' Paddy looked at Elizabeth rather hard. '*Do* you really want to?'

Elizabeth said that she did.

'And you will *be* there? Sometimes people don't always turn up.'

'I'll be there at half-past eight,' said Elizabeth.

'By the statue of Queen Victoria?'

'Yes.'

'And you won't forget to ask your mother about me coming to tea on Saturday?'

'Of course I won't,' said Elizabeth, shocked. 'I promised.'

'People don't always keep their promises,' said Paddy.

'Well *I* do,' said Elizabeth.

The first thing Mrs Muir wanted to know when she arrived indoors was whether she had come home with Sandra Gower.

'No,' said Elizabeth. 'I came home with someone else.'

'Did you? Well, that's good. You're obviously starting to find your feet. I told you it wouldn't take long, didn't I?'

'Yes,' said Elizabeth.

'Did you manage to talk to Sandra yet?'

'No. She doesn't sit near enough.' She felt like adding, 'And anyway, she's soppy . . .' but thought perhaps she'd better not. Mothers didn't like you saying that the daughters of other mothers were soppy; not when the mothers had coffee together. She'd found that out at Lady Margaret.

'Perhaps you'll have a chance tomorrow.' Mrs Muir set a plateful of chocolate pyramids on the table. 'Perhaps you might like to invite her back to tea some time.'

'Actually,' said Elizabeth, 'would it be all right if I asked someone else back to tea? On Saturday?'

'Saturday?' Mrs Muir looked doubtful. 'We really ought to go over and see Gran and Grandad on Saturday. We haven't been there for ages.'

'We could always go *next* Saturday,' said Elizabeth.

'Well . . . I suppose we could. If it's really important.'

'It *is* really important,' said Elizabeth. *'Honestly.'*

Mrs Muir laughed.

'Who have you invited? The Queen?'

Elizabeth scooped William off the floor and draped him over her shoulder, in the way that he liked.

'Paddy Dewar.'

'And who exactly is Paddy Dewar?'

'She's my best friend,' said Elizabeth.

4

'Can we have chocolate pyramids?' said Elizabeth. 'And meringues, as well?'

'Chocolate pyramids *and* meringues? My goodness gracious me! We are trying to impress.'

Elizabeth shuffled impatiently with her feet. Why did mothers always have to say these silly things? It wasn't in the *least* that she was trying to impress. It was simply that she didn't want to disappoint. Paddy had been eagerly plying her with questions all week: 'What do you usually do when people come to tea? Do you play games? Do you go out into the garden? What sort of things do you have to eat? Does your mother make fancy cakes? Does she do jellies, and things like that?' Elizabeth had assured her that she did; it would be terrible if just for once she didn't.

'You'd better tell me what else you want,' said Mrs Muir. 'I hadn't prepared myself for a banquet.'

'We could always have fudge fingers – or ginger-bread men. Or traffic lights! Could we have traffic lights?' Traffic lights were always a favourite: three different-coloured jellies – one strawberry, one orange, one lime – set into a bed of chocolate mousse. Even Jenny had liked traffic lights, and Jenny had been notoriously hard to please. Elizabeth looked at her mother, hopefully. *'Could* we?' she said.

'I daresay we might just about be able to run to it.'

'And the pyramids and the meringues?'

'Oh, and the pyramids and meringues ... all I can say is that Miss Paddy Dewar must obviously be a young person of no small consequence!'

'I told you,' said Elizabeth. 'She's my best friend.'

Paddy arrived promptly at two o'clock, which was the time they had arranged. Elizabeth, watching out of her bedroom window, saw her coming up the road and went running out to the gate to meet her. She was wearing the same skirt that she wore every day for school, navy blue pleats with a stain down the front where she'd slopped paint on it in an art class, but she'd changed out of her old grey sweater with the hole in the elbow and put on a bright cherry red one instead. Elizabeth was glad about that. Red suited her better than grey.

The first thing she said as Elizabeth opened the gate was: 'Is this your house? Isn't it lovely?'

Elizabeth was surprised.

'It's all right, I s'pose.'

'I think it's *lovely*,' said Paddy.

'The one we had before was much nicer.'

'Nicer than this?' Paddy sounded incredulous; as if she couldn't believe that anything *could* be nicer than Court Park Gardens.

'It was loads bigger,' said Elizabeth. She thought of Deepdene, with its sweeping gravel drive in front and the long back garden that merged into bluebell woods, where she and Timmy used to play. She wondered how anyone could think that Court Park Gardens was lovely. She had heard her father call it a biscuit tin. Her mother just said that it was 'compact'.

'Isn't it funny?' said Paddy. 'You went to a smaller

school and lived in a bigger *house* . . . now you go to a bigger *school* and live in a *smaller* house . . . is that your car? Isn't it beautiful?'

Elizabeth didn't say that the one they had had before was nicer, although she knew, now, that it *had* been. Her father was always sighing over it and saying, 'Oh, for my Armstrong Siddeley . . .' She'd asked him the other day why he didn't buy another one if he liked them so much, but he'd only twitched an eyebrow at her, rather irritably, and said, 'My dear Elizabeth, motor cars don't run on water, you know,' which hadn't really answered the question.

She took Paddy indoors to meet her mother. She had been rather anxious about this, lest Mrs Muir should make some belittling remark about preparing banquets or having the Queen to tea, but she needn't have worried. All her mother said was: 'Ah! So this is Paddy, is it? I gather you're quite an important personage, young lady?'

Afterwards, upstairs in Elizabeth's bedroom, Paddy confided to Elizabeth that she thought her mother was 'absolutely super'. Unlike Jenny, who had had a tendency to turn up her nose, Paddy was enthusiastic about everything and everyone; from William, who was 'the best looking cat I've ever seen' – Elizabeth fully agreed with her upon that – to Mr Muir, who was '*gorgeous*', which was rather more difficult to understand. Elizabeth loved her father, but she certainly wouldn't have described him as gorgeous. He had, as a matter of fact, been rather cross and unreasonable just lately, complaining about small, petty little things that would never have bothered him before, such as the television being left on when nobody was in the room and lights not being switched off when they should have been. He had also quite sharply informed Elizabeth that if she wanted a netball (she had wistfully mentioned the possibility) then she would have to save up her pocket money and buy one for herself. Either that or wait till Christmas.

'You've been a sight too spoiled, you two kids. From now on you're going to have to learn to moderate your demands. Learn to make sacrifices like the rest of us.'

She wouldn't have called *that* being very gorgeous. Still, it was always nice to know that one's parents were approved of, especially by one's best friend. Jenny had almost never approved of anything. The trouble had been that whatever Elizabeth had had, Jenny had always had as well; and anything that Jenny had was always bound to be bigger and better and three times more expensive. Even her parents had been superior, because Jenny's father was a Member of Parliament and was sometimes interviewed on the television, while Mr Muir only worked in an office, the same as everybody else.

'What does *your* father do?' she asked Paddy.

Paddy hesitated a second before replying.

'He's a film actor,' she said.

Elizabeth's eyes grew wide.

'*Really?*'

'Yes,' said Paddy. 'He makes films. In America. He's away making one now . . . are these books all yours? Aren't they *super*? Haven't you got a *lot*? Which is your favourite?'

Elizabeth said her favourite was *Little Women* – 'especially Jo and Laurie'. Paddy said that *Little Women* was her favourite, too.

53

'Except that I always think it's so mean,' said Elizabeth, 'that she doesn't let them get married.'

'Yes,' said Paddy. 'I think that's mean.'

'Amy's so *horrid*, and *spoilt.*'

'Yes,' said Paddy. 'She is, isn't she?'

'Jo's ever so much nicer.'

'I like Jo,' said Paddy. 'He's the one I like best of all.'

Elizabeth looked at her, doubtfully. She wondered if *Little Women* really was Paddy's favourite or if she was just saying it because she thought it was what Elizabeth would like to hear.

'Jo's not a boy,' she said. 'She's a girl.'

Beneath her freckles, Paddy grew pink.

'Yes, of course. I was getting her muddled up. It's ages since I read it. Ages and ages. Not since I was about – about *five*. I expect I've forgotten lots of it.'

Elizabeth felt mean; even meaner than Louisa M. Alcott not letting Jo and Laurie get married. After a moment's inner struggle, she said: 'You could borrow it, if you wanted.'

'*Could* I?' said Paddy.

Elizabeth struggled again. She hated lending her books. The last time she'd lent one it had come back all dog-eared and dirty. She'd sworn, then, that she would never lend one again. *Ever*, to *anyone*. But Paddy wasn't just anyone, was she? She was her best friend, and if you couldn't lend a book to your own best friend then it couldn't be very much of a friendship. Swallowing rather hard, she took down her copy of *Little Women*, with it's beautiful red covers that looked like real leather, and held it out.

'Here you are,' she said.

'Gosh, *thanks*,' said Paddy. 'I'll give it back to you,

54

I promise. I always give things back . . . are these all your ornaments? Aren't they super? Can I touch them?'

Elizabeth had a whole shelf full of ornaments. Mostly they were cats and dogs, but there was also a glass elephant, which her father had brought back from Brussels when he had gone there on a business trip, a china money pig with some old sixpenny pieces inside it, a bar of soap in the shape of a cow, which she could never bring herself to use, and her Victorian paperweight. The paperweight was a glass ball with two tiny figures inside it, a boy wearing old-fashioned knickerbockers and a muffler and a girl in a red cloak and a tartan beret with a pom-pom. They were collecting Christmas holly, with a small black dog romping at their side and a robin sitting on the branch of a nearby fir tree. The ground was covered in snow, and when you turned the paperweight upside down all the snow went swirling about in great white flakes, so that it looked as if there were a snowstorm.

Paddy was fascinated by it. She kept picking it up and shaking it, and watching as the eddying snowflakes sank slowly back to earth. Sometimes one or two would land on the girl's beret, or nestle in the boy's hair, which was long and golden, and that meant she had to shake it again, to dislodge them.

'It's ever so heavy,' she said.

'That's because it's a paperweight,' said Elizabeth. 'It was my great-grandmother's. She left it to me in her will when she died. It's over a hundred years old.'

Paddy set it back, reverently, upon the shelf.

'It must be ever so valuable.'

'I think it is, quite. But I wouldn't sell it. Mummy says I've got to keep it so that one day I can leave it to *my* grandchildren.'

They giggled at the thought of ever having grandchildren. They couldn't even imagine having children – couldn't even imagine being grown up.

'There's years and *years* to go yet,' said Paddy. 'You can't even leave school till you're sixteen.'

'I'm not going to leave till I'm eighteen,' said Elizabeth, 'and then I'm going to university. At least,' she added, suddenly remembering what Miss Hutton used to say about pride coming before a fall, 'I am if I'm clever enough.'

'I bet you will be,' said Paddy. 'You're ever so much cleverer than Julie Christmas, and *she's* the cleverest person in the whole class.'

Elizabeth frowned.

'It's not that I'm cleverer. It's just that at Lady Margaret we were more advanced.'

'It must have been a *super* school,' said Paddy.

'Yes, it was, but there were lots of things it didn't have that Gladeside has.'

She could afford to be generous now; having Paddy for a friend had made all the difference in the world. Gladeside at the end of the week didn't seem anywhere near as horrid as it had at the beginning. She felt that people didn't hate her any more. Julie Christmas, admittedly, was still a bit inclined to be standoffish, because Elizabeth could answer questions in French that she couldn't, even though she always let her have first go; but the boy called Sammy English had obviously forgiven her for criticizing his essay because he'd come up to her just before civics on Wednesday and said, ''Ere, quick, before old 'yslop catches us . . . whereja put the commas 'n fings in this lot, then?' and when she'd shown him he'd grinned and said 'Cor! Looks dead classy, dunnit?' and had seemed really pleased. Jo Ann, though remaining wary, had started to include her in her netball games, and on Friday morning the great John Diamond, who was the handsomest boy in the class, had actually smiled at her and said 'Hi' when they found themselves entering the school gates together. It was almost the best moment she had had so far.

Paddy, who was peering with one eye closed through the slit in the money box pig, said: 'What sort of things didn't your old school have that Gladeside has?'

'Well, it didn't have a swimming pool,' said Elizabeth, 'and it didn't have a sports field and it didn't have a sixth form, either. Not a proper one. I'd have had to go somewhere else when I got to sixteen in any case.'

'Did it have a uniform?' said Paddy, putting down the money box pig and picking up the elephant. 'What colour was it?'

'Brown and gold,' said Elizabeth. She seemed to remember that she had told Paddy that before.

'Was it nice?' said Paddy. 'Have you still got it? Can I see?'

Elizabeth opened the door of her wardrobe and showed her the brown blazer with the gold braid round the edges and the gold-and-brown quartered beret.

'Can I try it on?' said Paddy, eagerly. 'Oh! It's *super*! Oh, I *wish* we had uniforms at Gladeside . . . what's this say on the badge?'

'Ora et Labora,' said Elizabeth. 'It's Latin. It means, pray and work.'

'It's ever so lovely,' said Paddy. She stroked a finger down the embossed crest. 'I'd *love* to have a uniform. Specially one like this . . . this little beret thing is *super*.'

Overcome by sudden recklessness, Elizabeth said: 'You can have it, if you like.'

Paddy's face turned scarlet.

'*Can* I? *Honestly?* D'you mean it?'

For just a second, Elizabeth wondered if she really ought; and then she thought, it's only a *beret*. It wasn't as if she were giving the blazer away. She could see there might be some objections to that. But surely no one could object to her giving away a mere *beret*?

'I don't see why you shouldn't have it,' she said. 'I won't be wearing it any more. And anyway, it suits you better than it does me.'

'Gosh, *thanks*,' said Paddy.

'You'd better leave it up here with *Little Women*. We can collect them later. I expect we ought to go down now. I think it's probably tea time.'

Tea, with chocolate pyramids *and* meringues *and* traffic lights, was voted 'the nicest, nicest meal I've ever had'. Mrs Muir laughed, but seemed pleased. Mr Muir said: 'Would that everyone in this house were so easily satisfied.' Elizabeth knew that he was referring to her. He had told her only that morning that she should consider herself lucky she had a roof over her head and enough food to keep from starving.

'If you were a Vietnamese peasant, you'd think you were in paradise.'

It seemed such a silly remark to make – after all,

she *wasn't* a Vietnamese peasant, so what was the point? In any case, it wasn't fair: all she'd wanted was a netball.

Afterwards, when they went out into the garden to play with Timmy, Paddy said: 'I think your father is ever so lovely.'

'*Do* you?' said Elizabeth.

'Don't you?' said Paddy.

Elizabeth had never given the question very much thought.

'I s'pose he's all right really,' she said.

'I think he's lovely,' said Paddy.

'He used to be ever so much nicer. When we lived in Caterham. He never used to grumble, or say you couldn't have things. Now he does it all the time . . . Mummy says it's because of his new job.'

'Is he something important?' said Paddy.

Elizabeth didn't really know. She didn't really know what her father was.

'He's in an office,' she said.

Paddy nodded, wisely.

'I expect he's a managing director.'

'Mm . . .' Elizabeth was dubious. 'Maybe.'

'I expect he is,' said Paddy.

'No, he's not, he's a *space*man!' Adorned with a flower pot on his head and brandishing a hand fork, Timmy came hurtling joyously out of the garden shed. 'He's a *space*man and he travels to the *moon*!'

Elizabeth was just on the point of telling him that he oughtn't to help himself to things from the garden shed (last time he'd done it he had nearly chopped off his fingers trying to cut the lawn with a pair of hedge clippers) when Paddy said, 'Ooh, look! There's a wheelbarrow!' and pounced on it. 'Let's put Timmy inside it and play at being charioteers like in *Ben Hur*!'

'All right,' said Elizabeth.

For half an hour they played at being charioteers. Twice they crashed into the fence, and once they ran out of control and fell into a flower bed, and in the end the wheel came off the wheelbarrow, which made Elizabeth a trifle apprehensive, but Timmy enjoyed it and maybe nobody would ever notice that the fence had scrape marks on it and that some of the flowers were a bit crushed. Or if they did, then maybe they'd think it was a marauding cat, or someone's dog got in by mistake. She and Timmy didn't usually play games like that in the garden. At Deepdene they'd always gone down to the woody part at the end, where it didn't matter what damage they did. Here in Court Park Gardens there wasn't any woody part.

Paddy said: 'Will they be angry? About the wheelbarrow?'

'I don't know,' said Elizabeth. Normally she would have said no, and wouldn't have hesitated to own up; but with her father in the mood he'd been in just recently she wasn't too sure. It was quite possible that he would be very angry indeed and even stop her pocket money. He'd already threatened it once or twice, if she didn't learn to turn lights off. 'Let's put it in the shed and not mention it,' she said to Timmy. 'If they ask, we'll tell them; but if they don't we won't say anything.'

When Timmy had gone to bed, they all sat down to a game of Scrabble. Even her father joined in. He liked Scrabble, because he said it was educational. Paddy had never played before, but it didn't take her

61

long to master the rules. She was soon thinking of all the words she could which used Xs and Qs, and scheming along with the rest of them for double- and even triple-word scores. At one point she grew excited and shouted, 'Oh, *knickers*!' and then, a few seconds later: '*BLAST!*' It was perfectly understandable, because they'd reached the stage where there were only three letters left to be picked, one of which was an X, which Paddy had been waiting for for ages to make the word 'exit', which would have given her forty-five points and put her in the lead. Instead, she picked up an A, which was useless. Anyone might have shouted blast in the stress of such a moment. All the same, Elizabeth wished that she hadn't. Her parents were very strict about swearing. She saw them exchanging glances, then Mr Muir, reaching out for a letter, said: 'Now, then, young lady! We don't want any of that sort of language.' He said it quite mildly, but Elizabeth knew that he wasn't pleased.

She bent her head, cheeks glowing red with confusion. Jenny would never have sworn. Her parents had liked Jenny. They had always said that she was nicely behaved and had charming manners. But then Jenny, she reminded herself, had done nothing but run things down and pick holes – not in her parents' hearing, of course. Out in the garden, or next day at school.

'William isn't a real *thoroughbred* cat, is he?' she'd say. 'Ming's a Siamese: they're the most intelligent.'

Or else:

'Isn't your mother worried that Timmy can't read yet? I've got a cousin who's only three and a half, and he can read anything.'

62

Jenny had never said that her father was lovely, or admired her books and ornaments. *She* had even tried to be grudging about the Victorian paperweight.

'Of course,' she'd said, 'Victorian isn't *really* old. Not like Georgian. Our house is Georgian. It was built in *seventeen ninety-three.*'

Really, when she looked back on it, she hadn't actually liked Jenny very much. She did like Paddy, even though she'd said knickers and blast. After all, blast wasn't such a very bad thing to say. It wasn't like Christ or bloody.

At half-past seven, which was when Paddy had to go, Elizabeth smuggled a plastic carrier bag upstairs and wrapped up *Little Women* and her Lady Margaret beret. She was almost certain that her mother would say yes if she asked her, but there was just the little niggling doubt that for some reason of her own she might choose to say no. She wouldn't be able to bear it if she said no; not after promising.

Galloping back down the stairs, she thrust the carrier bag, rather breathlessly, at Paddy.

'Here you are! Take it.'

'Gosh, *thanks,*' said Paddy. 'I'll let you have the bag back.'

'You needn't bother about the bag,' said Elizabeth. 'We've got dozens.'

'But it's a good one.'

Elizabeth looked at it. It was just an ordinary, everyday carrier bag. Blue plastic, with 'GRANTS OF CROYDON' written across it in white lettering.

'Honestly,' she said, 'we've got loads.'

'Loads of what?' said her mother, coming into the hall to say goodbye.

'Carrier bags. I've given one to Paddy to carry *Little Women* in. She's borrowing it to read.'

'I'll be *ever* so careful with it,' said Paddy. 'And I will give it back, I promise. I always give things back.'

'Good gracious me,' said Mrs Muir, 'I'm sure you do! Well, Paddy—' She opened the front door. 'I'm glad you were able to come. I hope that you've enjoyed yourself.'

When Jenny and Elizabeth had gone to tea with each other, the last thing they had always said was, 'Thank you very much for having me,' because that was what they had been taught was correct. Paddy didn't say thank you very much for having me. What Paddy said was: 'It's been one of the *superest* times I've ever had. Can I come again?'

Mrs Muir laughed and said: 'Yes, I should think that you might . . . just so long as you remember not to bring any more naughty words with you!'

Elizabeth wanted to crawl under the front-door mat and die. If she had been Paddy, she wouldn't have known where to look. She hardly knew where to look even as it was. How could her mother be so *awful*?

Paddy, unlike Elizabeth, didn't seem in the least bit embarrassed.

'I'll remember,' she said, earnestly. 'Honestly, I promise. I won't ever say it again. I think your house is *lovely*. It's the nicest house I've ever been in.'

'Is it, indeed?' said Mrs Muir. 'Well, then, you must certainly come again. But I understand Elizabeth is going to come to you first. Is that right?'

'Yes,' said Paddy. 'But it's not nearly as nice as yours. Yours is *lovely*.'

When Paddy had finally gone, and the front door was closed, Mrs Muir said: 'What does Paddy's father do, do you know?'

'He's a film actor,' said Elizabeth.

Mrs Muir raised both eyebrows.

'A *film* actor? Well! I suppose that would account for it . . .'

5

On Monday morning, Paddy arrived at school carrying her books in the Grants of Croydon bag and wearing Elizabeth's old Lady Margaret beret with a teddy bear brooch pinned over the badge. Elizabeth didn't like to say anything, but she couldn't help hoping that none of the staff from Lady Margaret caught sight of it. She wasn't sure how they would feel about someone from another school wearing one of their berets in public, especially with a teddy bear brooch pinned on to the front.

Paddy announced proudly that she had spent all day Sunday reading *Little Women*, which she had brought with her in the carrier bag. She was almost halfway through it. She thought that Jo was 'super' and agreed with Elizabeth that Amy was 'horrid and stuck up'.

'She gets better when she's married,' said Elizabeth. 'That's in *Good Wives* . . . I'll lend you that when you've finished *Little Women*, if you like.'

In English that morning Mrs Hyslop told them that for homework they were to write a short paragraph describing some object of their own choosing, but without actually saying what the object was.

'The idea is that the way you describe it should be sufficiently clear for the rest of us to guess. Obviously you don't want to choose anything *too* easy, or there wouldn't be any fun in it – you'd only have to mention the word "screen", for instance, and we'd all know at once you were talking about a television set. Try to choose something that's interesting and unusual without being too obscure – and if it's something fairly small, so that you can bring it along to show us, then so much the better.'

Elizabeth chose her Victorian paperweight. She started off her paragraph with, 'This object is a transparent glass sphere about the size of a tennis ball,' and she ended up, 'It is over one hundred years old but is more than just a toy as it is also useful, owing to the weight of it.' She knew that Paddy would recognize it at once, but she would put Paddy on her honour not to say anything until everyone else had had a go. She would be very surprised if they managed to guess.

The paragraphs were to be read out in class on Wednesday. Elizabeth spent Tuesday evening wrestling with the problem of whether or not she ought to ask her mother if it would be all right for her to take the paperweight to school. In the end, she decided that she wouldn't bother. She would just take it. It was her paperweight, after all. You didn't need permission to take your own things about with you. She felt a bit guilty, nonetheless, as she packed it away in her bag next morning, underneath her school books.

English was the first class after break. It was a double period, which meant they had over an hour, but even so Mrs Hyslop said they wouldn't be able to read out all the paragraphs that morning. She said they would read half that morning, and half the following week.

'We'll start at the top of the register, with the As—'
Elizabeth's heart sank: she had been looking forward
to reading her paragraph *today*, not next week '—and
we'll work our way through the alphabet taking
alternate letters . . . A, C, E, etc. All right?'

Elizabeth ran quickly through the alphabet on her
fingers, beneath the desk. A(b)C(d)E(f)G(h)I(j)
K(l)M – *M*! She sat back, beaming.

'So,' said Mrs Hyslop. 'Let's start off with A for
Armstrong . . . what have you got for us, Michael?'

Michael Armstrong had described a model aero-
plane: everyone guessed it immediately, before he
had even finished the first sentence. It was silly,
thought Elizabeth, to say straight out that something
was made of Balsa wood and was ten inches long and
had two wings and a cockpit. It made it far too
simple. If you were going to describe something
ordinary and everyday, then you had to make sure
that the description was clever.

Most people *had* described things that were fairly
ordinary, except for Julie Christmas, who had
described a photograph of herself wearing a ballet
dress, which she took great pleasure in passing round
for everyone to look at (though not before they had all
guessed what it was) and Sammy English, who had
described a chocolate digestive, which he said was
'round and flat, with dimples on its bottom and a
brown cover on top'. Everyone had laughed, but no
one had been able to guess what he was talking
about. When they had all given up, including Mrs
Hyslop, he had produced it from his pocket with a
triumphant flourish, and then, with an even more
triumphant flourish, put it in his mouth and started
eating it. Mrs Hyslop had said: 'All right, Sammy . . .

one up to you. Just don't think you can get away with it twice, that's all!'

At last, after an agonizing period of suspense – would they get as far as her or would they not? – it came to Elizabeth's turn. Paddy, who had already been sworn to strictest secrecy, managed to sit in silence (apart from the odd excited squeak of recognition) while she read, but immediately afterwards couldn't help bursting out with, 'I know what it is, because I've seen it!'

'Then it wouldn't be fair for you to guess, would it?' said Mrs Hyslop. 'Let's find out if anyone else has any ideas.'

Janet Newman, who was Julie Christmas's best friend, thought it might be a crystal ball, 'like fortune tellers use'. Someone else thought it was 'one of those things you look in and see pictures'. Mrs Hyslop said: 'I think *I* know what it is – and if I'm right, then it must be very lovely. It's a paperweight, isn't it?'

'It's *Victorian*,' said Paddy. 'Her great-grandmother left it to her in her will.'

'Did she really?' said Mrs Hyslop. 'Well, Elizabeth, you are a lucky girl. It's not everyone can boast a genuine Victorian paperweight. I'd be very interested to see it. I don't suppose you've been able to bring it in to school with you?'

Shyly, Elizabeth nodded and produced it from her desk.

'Well, that *is* beautiful.' Mrs Hyslop came down the gangway to look at it more closely. 'A real Victorian paperweight!'

'Turn it upside down,' urged Paddy.

Mrs Hyslop did so.

'Oh, yes! Quite a snowstorm.' All the class craned

69

their necks to look. She held it up for them to see, then gently set it back again on Elizabeth's desk. 'You must take the greatest care of this,' she said. 'It's something very special.'

'She's going to keep it and give it to her own grandchildren,' said Paddy.

'Yes, that's an excellent idea . . . hand it down from generation to generation. That way it will become a family heirloom. Thank you very much for bringing it in to show us, Elizabeth. It's the most interesting object we've had all morning.'

When the bell rang for the end of class, Elizabeth found herself suddenly surrounded; everyone, it seemed, wanted to see the paperweight. Everyone wanted to hold it and turn it upside down and watch the snowflakes flying. People who had never even bothered to speak to her before jostled with each other for the privilege. Julie Christmas sniffed and said, 'They sell that sort of thing in Woolworth's,' but it didn't stop everyone else from being impressed. The girls mostly liked it for the little figures inside; the boys speculated what the snow was made of. Sammy English said it was probably bits of polystyrene, but as one of the others pointed out, they didn't have polystyrene in Victorian times. *He* thought it was most likely to be torn-up paper.

'Well, whatever it is,' said Jo Ann, 'it's really beautiful.' Elizabeth glowed: that was the first nice thing Jo Ann had ever said to her. She began to feel that she was really making headway.

At the end of the first class of the morning, which was RI, the boy Redmond appeared at her elbow. Elizabeth was a bit afraid of Redmond. He was huge and hulking, with a shock of fair hair and an

aggressive manner. He was always making the teachers' lives a misery by shouting, or stamping with his feet, or banging on his desk lid. Elizabeth wasn't in the least surprised that he had been 'caned more than any other boy in the whole school'. She was only surprised that he hadn't been expelled. Fortunately, he didn't turn up for every class, because for some of them he had to go away and do a thing called remedial, which Paddy said was for people who were backward. They had happily been spared his presence in English that morning, or they would never have been able to get as far through the alphabet as they had; Redmond would have seen to that. Now, glowering down at Elizabeth, he said: 'Where is it, then?'

Elizabeth swallowed.

'Where's what?'

'That thing you bin showin' everyone.'

'You mean the paperweight,' said Paddy.

'Yeah. The paperweight.'

'It's in my desk,' said Elizabeth. She took it out and cradled it protectively. 'I've got to take it home.'

Redmond held out a hand.

'Let's 'ave a butcher's.

Butcher's? Elizabeth was alarmed. What did he mean, butcher's? It sounded as if it might be something violent. She clutched more tightly at the paperweight.

Redmond, growing impatient, snapped his fingers.

'Come on, then! Let's 'ave a look.'

'*Please*,' said Paddy.

'You keep out of it,' said Redmond. 'It ain't your paperweight.'

'It's mine and Elizabeth's,' said Paddy, 'because we're friends and we share things. And we don't let just *any*one look at it.'

Redmond said something rude.

'Now you shan't see it at all,' said Paddy. '*Shall* he?' She turned, for confirmation, to Elizabeth. 'Not until he apologizes.'

'Oh, all *right*!' roared Redmond. 'I'm *sorry. Now* c'n I see it?'

'Only if you promise to be careful,' said Paddy. 'We don't want it broken.'

'I'll be *careful*,' said Redmond.

Reluctantly, Elizabeth passed him the paperweight. He studied it intently for a few moments, shook it, studied it again, then with a grunt handed it back.'

'Yeah,' he said. 'Not bad.'

'*Thank* you,' prompted Paddy.

Redmond said the same rude thing that he had said before, except that this time he stuck up two fingers to go with it.

'Really,' said Paddy, 'that boy is quite *horrid*.' She watched as he went shambling off in the wake of all the rest of the class. 'I don't think he *deserves* to look at our paperweight any more.'

News of the paperweight spread quickly. When Elizabeth came back to school after dinner (she always came back promptly now, so that she would have time for a game of netball before afternoon school; she was thinking of asking her mother whether she mightn't stay on and use the school canteen, the same as most of the others did) Paddy met her with the excited information that 'There are *dozens* of people who want to look at our paperweight . . . I keep telling them it's valuable and we can't show it to just *any*one, but they still keep on asking.'

All that afternoon, people kept asking. Girls – and even boys – from 1A and 1B, who had never taken the least bit of notice of her before, kept coming up to her and saying, 'Are you the one with the paperweight?' 'Are you the one that has that glass ball thing with the snowstorm inside it?' She had to disappoint them; the paperweight had been safely restored to her mantelshelf at home, standing in its customary position between the china money box pig and the cow made out of soap. She almost began to wish that she'd kept it at school with her. After all, people only wanted to look at it. Looking couldn't do any harm.

She had almost decided to bring it in with her again the next morning, but at the last minute, as she was about to push it into her case, her mother appeared in the doorway and said, 'Elizabeth, it's just starting to rain. You'd better get your raincoat'; and then, while she was getting it, stayed on to fuss about cat's hairs on the bedclothes and the cost of having blankets cleaned. Really, Elizabeth thought, her parents did nothing these days except *nag*. Who cared about a few cat's hairs? Cat's hairs didn't hurt anyone.

Because of the rain, they had to do PE that morning in the assembly hall, boys and girls together. Redmond, and Janet Newman, and John Diamond and the girl called Dawn Forrest, who was a Plymouth Brother, were told to pick teams for races. They had to pick boys and girls alternately, so that each team had a fair mix. John Diamond picked Paddy first of all, and then he picked Michael

74

Armstrong, and then he picked Elizabeth.' She could hardly believe it when she heard him say, 'I'll have Elizabeth.' She almost hesitated to go forward, in case there might be someone else by that name, but there wasn't. She was the only Elizabeth in the whole class, and John Diamond had picked her! She stood there, in line, in silent ecstasy, safe and secure as the numbers dwindled. Only eight people left – only four people left – only three, only two, only *one*. The very last to be chosen was poor Fat Spencer, who ate candles to show off. Paddy said she was always the last.

'She's so fat she can hardly even *move*.'

Elizabeth felt sorry for her. It must be dreadful being so fat, and so plain, and having to eat candles as a way of distinguishing yourself. It must be even *more* dreadful, always being the last person to be chosen. She would die of shame if she were ever the last.

The next-to-last was Sandra Gower, but she didn't feel sorry for her. Sandra Gower was just what Paddy had said she was: soppy. She not only spoke with a lisp, because her tongue was too long for her mouth (she had to practise Michael and Moses with it curled round a special steel knitting needle, which she was always trying to show people), she also put on airs and graces, aping Julie Christmas, the only difference being that Julie Christmas had something to put on airs and graces *about*, whereas Sandra Gower didn't. Julie Christmas was clever, and she was pretty, and she was popular. Sandra Gower wasn't any of those things; she was just dim. Not even just *dim*, but actually quite horrid. She had come up to Elizabeth earlier in the week and asked her if she would like to come to tea on Saturday.

'Mummy thayth I ought to invite you ath we live tho clothe and you're our thort of people.'

With grave politeness, Elizabeth had thanked her but said she was afraid she couldn't come this particular Saturday as she had to go and visit her grandparents in East Grinstead, and the Saturday after that she had already arranged to have tea with Paddy. At the mention of Paddy, Sandra Gower had curled her lip.

'Nobody hath tea with *her*. *My* mother wouldn't even let me *thpeak* to her.'

When Elizabeth in astonishment and indignation, had asked why not, Sandra had shrugged a shoulder and said: 'She'th not really our thort of perthon.'

Elizabeth had decided there and then that Sandra Gower wasn't *her* sort of person. It didn't seem that she was anyone else's, either, since the only friend she had in the whole class was Fat Spencer, who probably, Elizabeth thought, was not in much of a position to choose. She was glad that it was Fat who was in their team rather than Sandra, even if she *was* so enormous she could hardly move, which meant that the rest of them had to run twice as fast as anyone else if they were to stand any chance of winning. In fact, they did win, just once; they won the relay, and John Diamond said that it was largely due to Elizabeth.

'That was really great, the way you picked that baton up after Michael went and dropped it.'

'I told you she'd be good,' said Paddy.

Elizabeth knew, then, that it was only because of Paddy that John Diamond had chosen her. She didn't mind. She had at least been able to demonstrate to him that she was a useful person to have in a team. Next time, perhaps, he would choose her because *he* wanted her.

Later that day, as they were walking round the playground together, Paddy said: 'John Diamond likes you. He told me that he did.'

'Did he?' said Elizabeth, trying not to sound too eager.

'I asked him if he thought you were pretty, and he said yes . . . he thinks you're prettier even than Julie Christmas.'

Elizabeth wasn't quite sure whether she could believe this or not. She would have liked to believe it, naturally, but common sense told her that it couldn't possibly be true. Julie Christmas was one of the prettiest girls in the whole school; no one in their right mind would even begin to compare Elizabeth with her. She decided, regretfully, that it was just one of Paddy's well-meaning exaggerations – one of her ways of demonstrating loyalty. Still, it was nice that she was thought to be *quite* pretty, which was probably what John Diamond had actually said. There were some people who couldn't even be called *almost* pretty: some people who were just plain plain. She was glad she wasn't one of those.

'He wanted to know,' said Paddy, 'whether he could see our paperweight, 'cos he wasn't here yesterday and everyone's been telling him about it. I said you'd taken it back home, but that maybe we could bring it in again. I said I'd talk to you about it and see how we felt. Of course I told him that we couldn't keep showing it to just *any*one.'

But John Diamond wasn't just anyone, was he? He

was the handsomest boy in the class and he'd said that he liked her.

'I'll bring it with me first thing tomorrow morning,' promised Elizabeth.

'And we'll just let *him* see it,' said Paddy. 'Not people like Redmond. It'll get worn out if we keep letting people like Redmond have a go.'

Inevitably, people like Redmond did have a go. Word soon leaked out that Elizabeth had brought her paperweight to school again – even people who had seen it before kept wanting to have another look at it. It was really very difficult to refuse, especially when it was Jo Ann, or Sammy English. Sammy English had been almost friendly lately, ever since she'd shown him where to put his commas, and even Jo Ann was showing signs of a thaw. She wasn't going to risk antagonizing them again, she didn't care if the paperweight *was* Victorian or if it *had* been her great-grandmother's. It wasn't worth getting possessive about.

Paddy was the one who got possessive. Right from the very start she had adopted a proprietorial air towards the paperweight; now she protected it fiercely against all comers.

'Don't let him touch it,' she'd say scoldingly to Elizabeth. 'His hands are dirty . . . tell him he's got to go away and wash them. They'll wear it out, keeping on touching it all the time.'

In the end, it had become too much for her.

'You can't be *trusted* with it,' she said. 'You're letting just *any*one look at it.'

It didn't occur to Elizabeth to point out that as it was her paperweight she was entitled to let 'just anyone look at it', if that was what she wanted.

Meekly, she allowed Paddy to take it away from her and put it into her own desk.

'It'll be safer here,' said Paddy. '*I* won't let them all come mauling and clawing at it. If anyone wants to see it in future, they'll have to ask *me*.'

Somehow, after that, Elizabeth didn't like to say that she was going to take it home again – she felt that Paddy would be hurt if she were to remove it from her. In any case, she couldn't see any reason why it shouldn't be kept at school for people to look at. Her father was always saying that objects of beauty should be shared. Well, that was what she was doing: sharing her paperweight. With Paddy guarding it so jealously, it certainly wasn't going to come to any harm. All the same, she thought, she wouldn't tell her mother. Just in case.

6

Elizabeth felt mean when it came to Saturday and she was jumping into the back of the car with Timmy to drive out to East Grinstead and one of Gran's special cream teas, leaving Paddy behind in Croydon all by herself. Paddy had been disappointed when Elizabeth said she couldn't see her that weekend. She had wanted to know 'why not Sunday?' Elizabeth had tried to explain that Sunday wasn't possible because on Sunday Uncle Clive and Aunt Judith were coming over from Greenwich with Anne and Susan. Paddy had scowled and said: 'Who's Anne and Susan?'

'They're my cousins,' said Elizabeth.

'D'you see them often?'

'Quite often.'

'People are *always* going to see cousins . . . *cousins* and *grand*parents.'

'Don't you ever?' said Elizabeth.

'Haven't got any.'

'Haven't got *any*. Haven't got any at *all*?'

'Don't want any.'

'But they give you things! On Christmas, and birthdays . . . my grandmother always asks me what I want. Usually I say books, but this year I'm going to say a netball. Then I can bring it to school and we can make up our own gang.'

'Don't want a gang,' said Paddy. 'Gangs are *stupid*.'

'Well, then, we can just play by ourselves . . . we can practise shooting.'

'Don't like shooting,' said Paddy. She wasn't tall enough to be a shooter. Centre was the position she liked best.

'All right, then,' said Elizabeth. 'We can practise passing . . . I bet if we practised long enough you'd get into the Under-14s as easy as anything. You're heaps better than that Stopes girl. Everybody says so – even Jo Ann.'

Paddy just grunted, and refused to be solaced. Elizabeth wished she could have asked her to come with them – she was sure Gran and Grandad wouldn't have minded. Next time, she decided, that was what she would do. She would explain that she had this friend who had no grandparents of her own, and they would immediately say, 'In that case, you must bring her with you,' and then she would tell Paddy and Paddy would be all happy and pleased and her face would go into a big beaming smile, the way that it did when she was especially delighted by anything.

Towards the end of tea, Gran gave her the very opportunity she had been waiting for. She said: 'And how is the new school, Elizabeth? Have another cake, dear. I know you like them. Have you made any friends there yet?'

'I've made one,' said Elizabeth. Careful not to take the biggest, she helped herself to a pink-iced cake from the plate that Gran was holding out.

'Have you?' said Gran. 'What's her name?'

'Her name's Paddy.'

'And is she nice?'

'Yes,' said Elizabeth. She bit into her cake. 'I wish she could have come here today. She'd have liked to come here. She hasn't got any grandparents of her own.'

She waited for Gran to say, 'Really? Then the next time you must bring her along with you' – which was exactly what Gran *would* have said – but Mrs Muir broke in instead with: 'You make her sound like a foundling! I'm sure she's got a mother and father and a perfectly good home.'

'Yes, but she hasn't any *grand*parents,' said Elizabeth.

'Well, not everyone is so lucky – and don't talk with your mouth full. Timmy, remove those elbows from the table! How many more times must I tell you? Elizabeth, why don't you eat up what's on your plate and take him out into the garden with you? That would be much the best idea – and just make sure you watch Grandad's flower beds!'

She was alarmed at the mention of flower beds. Did that mean that they had noticed? She had been hoping they would put it down to stray cats. At least (cross fingers) they didn't seem to have found the wheelbarrow . . .

The wheelbarrow was yet to come. On Sunday morning, Mr Muir did some gardening. Elizabeth was upstairs in her bedroom, writing about the Battle of Hastings for history. At lunch, which was early, because of Uncle Clive and Aunt Judith coming, Mrs Muir said: 'Is there anyone here, I wonder, who can tell me anything about a broken wheelbarrow?' Elizabeth turned pink, but before she could say anything, Timmy's voice had gone shrilling across the table: 'She said we weren't to say!'

'I didn't!' Elizabeth was indignant.

'You did!'

'I didn't!'

'You did!'

'I *didn't*! I said —' She floundered.

'You said we wasn't to!'

'I said we would if anybody *asked*.'

'Well!' said Mrs Muir. 'And now somebody has . . . so now what have you got to say?'

'*She* did it,' said Timmy.

'I wasn't asking you, young man! I was talking to Elizabeth.'

Elizabeth hung her head.

'It was an accident.'

'Then why on earth didn't you come and tell me? You know we're never angry if you own up. Just putting it away as it was and leaving us to find out wasn't a very nice trick, was it?'

Elizabeth was silent.

'We was playin' Rom'n chariots,' said Timmy. (He pronounced it 'char-yuts'.)

'I see! That was last Saturday, I presume? When you were making all the noise and falling into flower beds? *And* I see the fence has been scraped. Heaven only knows what you did there.'

'It was the char-yut,' said Timmy.

'You mean, the wheelbarrow.'

'Yes, 'n 'Lizbeth 'n that girl that came kept runnin' too fast 'n bumpin' me into things.'

'Oh, don't be such a *sneak*,' said Elizabeth, infuriated. 'You enjoyed it.'

'No, I didn'.'

83

'Yes, you did!'

'No, I *did*—'

'WILL YOU BE QUIET, THE PAIR OF YOU!'

That was Mr Muir, banging on the table. William, who had been crouched in secretive fashion over the gravy boat, helping himself when he thought that nobody was looking, sprang up in guilty panic. Gravy boat and water jug went flying. William, wisely, disappeared (to be found, half an hour later, sitting fatly on the front-room window sill wiping gravy off his whiskers). Elizabeth wished that she could disappear, too. She hated it when people were cross with her. She didn't know which was worse: when they were cross and you deserved it, or when they were cross and you didn't. The second made you feel more hard-done-by, but the first meant that sooner or later you had to apologize. She supposed that sooner or later she would have to apologize about the beastly wheelbarrow.

'I really am very hurt,' said Mrs Muir, mopping gravy with one cloth and water with the other, 'that you could do such a thing and not tell us.'

It would have been easier if Timmy weren't there. She hated having to apologize in front of him.

'It really does upset me,' said Mrs Muir.

There was a pause, while everyone waited.

'Sorry,' said Elizabeth.

'Well, just so long as you are.' Mrs Muir went through to the kitchen with her gravy-and-water-soaked cloths. 'You've always been such a truthful girl. I shouldn't like to think that you were becoming deceitful.'

As if the wheelbarrow wasn't enough, Mrs Muir found out, during the week, about the missing beret.

When Elizabeth came home from school on Wednesday afternoon, she asked her where it was.

'I've been searching high and low for it. I've got the blazer, but I can't find the beret anywhere. I know we brought it with us, because I remember seeing it. It was there, in your wardrobe. You haven't taken it to school or anything, have you?'

Elizabeth's stomach turned a slow somersault. She knew a moment's temptation to deny all knowledge – to say that she had lost it, left it on a bus, had it stolen; but the moment passed, and it was too late. Cheeks scarlet, she said: 'I gave it to Paddy.'

'Gave it to Paddy?' Her mother repeated the words in astonishment and disbelief. 'Gave her your *beret*? What on earth for?'

Elizabeth swallowed.

'I didn't think we wanted it any more.'

'Oh! So *you* didn't think we wanted it any more? I suppose it didn't occur to you to ask *me* whether we wanted it any more?'

Elizabeth made a small mumbling noise.

'As it so happens,' said Mrs Muir, 'that beret would have come in extremely useful. I had Jenny's mother on the telephone this morning, asking me if by any chance we'd hung on to things like berets and blazers—'

'*Jenny's* mother?' said Elizabeth.

'Yes! Jenny's mother! She's got a niece who's starting at Lady Margaret next term. I told her she'd be very welcome to have both your blazer and your beret – and now I find you've gone and given one of them away without even asking me! You really are becoming very naughty. You must have known perfectly well that you should have checked with me first. What did the child want it for, anyway? She can't wear it. All she can use it for is dressing up. It's just a sheer waste! It could be going to someone who really needs it. School uniforms cost a great deal of money, you know.'

'Yes,' said Elizabeth.

'I really am very angry with you. I don't suppose it's the least bit of use asking the child to give it back; she's bound to have ruined it by now. Judging from the state of the rest of her clothes, nothing would last more than five minutes. Really, Elizabeth, I'm not at all pleased.'

She was expecting another apology. That would be the second one in only four days. Elizabeth couldn't bring herself to do it – the word 'sorry' just wouldn't come. Even now she honestly couldn't see what she had done that was so very wrong. After all, it was *her* beret, and she would much rather Paddy had it than Jenny's mother. She didn't like Jenny's mother: she was loud and bossy and wore horrid fur coats that had once belonged to animals. She was *glad* she couldn't have the beret. It was bad enough that she was going to have the blazer.

'I don't know,' said Mrs Muir. She shook her head. 'I just do not know what has come over you lately . . . you break things and you don't tell us, you trample down the flower beds, you ruin the fence, now you're giving your clothes away without permission. You never used to behave like this. What's the matter with you?' She went on without waiting for an answer: 'All I can say is, you'd better pull your socks up, my girl, or you and I are going to have a serious talk together.'

Thought we'd just had one, thought Elizabeth;

but she didn't say so. If her mother was going to start being as cross and unreasonable as her father had become, life was going to be pretty well un*bear*able.

On Friday afternoon as they left school, Paddy said: 'You are coming tomorrow, aren't you? You do *promise* that you are? You won't suddenly *not* come at the last minute?'

'Of course I won't,' said Elizabeth, shocked. 'I don't do things like that.'

She set off for Paddy's directly after lunch the next day.

'Don't forget,' said Mrs Muir, as she left. 'I want you home no later than six.'

'All right,' said Elizabeth.

Paddy lived in one of the tiniest cottages that anyone had ever seen. It was the middle one of a row of five, down in West Croydon, near the railway line. Over the door it said 'Tansy Cottages, 1834.' That wasn't as old as Jenny's house had been, but still, thought Elizabeth, it was old. Eighteen thirty-four was older than Victoria, because Victoria hadn't come to the throne until eighteen thirty-seven. It was awe-inspiring to think that when you stepped over the doorstep you were stepping where real people out of history had stepped – men and women from other ages, who had actually walked over that very threshold and into that very same hall.

'I wish we lived in an old house,' she said.

'Your house is *lovely*,' said Paddy. 'I'd *much* rather live in yours.'

Just at first, Elizabeth couldn't possibly imagine how she could say so. To her, No. 3 Tansy Cottages was a delight. It was like a dolls' house. You opened

the front door, and there were the stairs, right in front
of you, narrow as a stepladder, going straight up into
the bedroom. Downstairs, there was a tiny little dark
passage with two tiny little rooms opening off it –
rooms that were so extremely tiny that Elizabeth felt
like a great clumping giant banging about in them.
She was sure if she went on tiptoe and stretched, she
would be able to touch the ceilings with her fingertips. Beyond the second of the two rooms was a sort of
lean-to, all covered in glass, which served as a
kitchen. On the glass, moss was growing, and birds
had left their droppings. Elizabeth didn't mind the
droppings; she thought only what fun it must be in
the depths of winter to throw nuts and pieces of bread
up there and watch the starlings and the blue tits
feeding, just a foot away from you, overhead.

Later, when she stopped to think about it, she
realized that there *would* be disadvantages, living in a
place so very old and so very small. Because there
was only the one bedroom, Paddy had to share it
with her mother; they both slept together in a big
iron bedstead which took up almost three-quarters of
the floor space. (Elizabeth wondered what happened
when Mr Dewar came back from making his films.
Perhaps Paddy slept downstairs on a camp bed?)
The bathroom, which had been built on as an after-
thought, because in 1834 ordinary people didn't
have such luxuries, opened off the bedroom and was
just large enough to accommodate an old-fashioned
washbasin and a funny, green-painted bath tub with
tall sides. (The lavatory was in the back yard, which
Elizabeth couldn't help thinking would be rather
spooky on a cold, dark winter's night.) In one corner
of the bedroom ceiling there was a large stain where

the roof leaked, owing to some of the tiles having fallen off, and downstairs in the front room the wallpaper was peeling and had had to be tacked back on with drawing pins.

'It's the damp,' said Paddy. 'Doesn't matter how often you nag at them, they still won't do anything about it. My mum's down the town hall twice a week asking them. They just tell her to go away again and stop being a nuisance.'

'Who do?' said Elizabeth, confused.

'The council. Down the town hall. They're ever so rotten to her. They make her cry. Sometimes she gets mad and says she'd like to put a bomb under them.'

Elizabeth was alarmed. She couldn't imagine a mother crying, or wanting to put bombs under people. Nervously, she said: 'Where is she now? Your mother?'

'Down the market. She always goes down the market Saturday afternoon. You get things cheaper. D'you want to come for a walk? I'll show you a haunted house, if you like.'

'All right,' said Elizabeth.

The haunted house was in the next street. It had once been a solid Victorian residence, standing in detached splendour in its own acres of garden. Now it was deserted, the garden derelict and overgrown. All the doors and windows of the house had been boarded up, and a high wooden fence erected to keep out intruders. Elizabeth, peering at the dismal scene through a spyhole, was startled to hear Paddy say: 'D'you want to climb over?

Elizabeth looked at her, doubtfully.

'Climb over the fence?'

'Yes – so's we can go inside. Have a look round.'

'But it says it's a dangerous structure—'

'That's only to keep people out.' Paddy spoke with careless confidence. 'It doesn't mean anything.'

'But ought we to?' said Elizabeth. The notice pinned to the fence quite plainly said *PRIVATE* and *Trespassers will be Prosecuted*. 'S'pose someone sees us?'

'Who cares?' said Paddy. 'I've been in lots of times. Lots and *lots* of times . . . c'mon!'

Already she was pulling herself up, and over the top. Elizabeth, who was by nature law abiding, followed somewhat apprehensively.

'It's easy!' called Paddy. 'Just jump!'

Elizabeth jumped. As she fell, she grazed her knee on something hard, and ripped the hem of her dress on something sharp; but at least she was down. At least she was behind the fence, where nobody could see her and call the police to come and start prosecuting.

They spent all afternoon exploring the haunted house. They didn't come across any ghosts (for which Elizabeth was secretly glad) but they poked about in the attics and they grubbed around in the cellars, they peered up chimney stacks, investigated under loose floorboards, picked over rubbish that had been left behind in cupboards. Paddy, the adventurous, slid down the banisters from the top of the house almost to the bottom; Elizabeth, less bold, slid down them halfway and got a splinter in her leg. Outside in the overgrown garden they blazed trails to far-off places. Paddy, clambering up a horse chestnut tree to survey the landscape, missed her footing and fell plop into a bed of stinging things, while Elizabeth, forgetting to be cautious, stepped on what looked like a patch of bright green grass only to

90

PRIVATE

TRESPASSERS WILL

BE   PROSECUTED

find herself knee deep in a pool of stagnant water. She hadn't terribly minded about the splinter or the grazed knee, but the sensation of cold, clammy, clinging dampness in her shoes was something different. Apart from anything else, it smelt horrid. Just for a moment, her lip quivered. The thought of having to spend the rest of the afternoon *smelling*, in wet shoes and socks—

'It's all right,' said Paddy. 'You can have mine.'

Elizabeth tried to protest, but Paddy could be obstinate. She said that if she wanted to go barefoot for a friend, then she would do so; that was what friendship was all about. Fortunately, it didn't quite come to that, because Elizabeth's feet were longer than Paddy's and wouldn't cram into her sandals no matter how hard she tried, so that in the end she just wore Paddy's socks inside her own wet shoes, while Paddy went barefoot in her sandals.

When they arrived back at No. 3 Tansy Cottages, Paddy's mother was there. She didn't look like a woman who would want to put bombs under people. She looked far too frail and fragile ever to do anything violent. She had a small, pixie-ish face like Paddy's, except that it was thinner and paler – everything about Mrs Dewar was thin and pale: her hair (which curled quite prettily), her hands, her arms, even her clothes. She looked worn and tired, as if she had some permanent worry in life – the fact, perhaps, thought Elizabeth, that her husband was always away making films while she had to stay here with damp patches on the bedroom ceiling and the wallpaper peeling off the front-room wall, all because the people at the town hall wouldn't do anything about it and kept making her cry. Elizabeth found herself feeling sorry for her. It was rather disturbing, because you didn't expect to feel sorry for people's mothers.

When she saw Elizabeth, Mrs Dewar said: 'Oh, dear! How cross your mother will be! Just look at the mess you're in! Whatever shall we do?'

Paddy suggested they boil a kettle of water and take it up to the bathroom to have a wash. Mrs Dewar said: 'Yes – I suppose – but it's no use. It'll never come out. That green stuff never does. Oh, dear! This is dreadful! I do hope it wasn't a new dress?'

As a matter of fact it was, fairly, but Elizabeth didn't like to say so. She was terrified that Paddy's mother might burst into tears if she said it had been bought only two months ago and had hardly as yet been worn. She said: 'No, it's nothing particularly special.'

'In any case, she's got *hundreds*,' said Paddy. 'You ought to see her wardrobe . . . she's got *loads*.'

Mrs Dewar seemed slightly comforted at this. By the time they returned from the bathroom (the green stains, as predicted, had not come out – if anything, they had been made even worse) tea had been laid on a table in the back room. Mrs Dewar kept apologizing for the fact that 'I can't compete with what you gave Paddy. I've heard all about what a wonderful meal she had. All the pretty cakes. All the jellies. I can't compete with that. I'm afraid you'll find this very dull and boring.' Elizabeth felt embarrassed. She began to wonder whether perhaps chocolate pyramids *and* meringues *and* traffic lights might not have been rather showy and vulgar. Bread and jam and Wagon Wheels would have tasted just as nice – maybe even nicer. Certainly in the tiny back room at No. 3 Tansy Cottages they did. She wasn't finding them in the least bit dull or boring. She tried to say as much to Paddy's mother, but Mrs Dewar only sighed and shook her head and said: 'I can't compete. I know it's not what your used to, but I'm afraid it's the best I can do.'

After tea, Paddy and Elizabeth went out into the back yard to feed Paddy's rabbit, who was called Clarence. He was large, and white, and fluffy, and they played with him for a long time, until somewhere, suddenly, a church clock began striking the hour: it was six o'clock, and Elizabeth should have been back home. Mrs Dewar became very upset and flustered when she heard.

'This is terrible! What will your mother say? You must telephone her at once! There's a call box at the end of the road. You must stop off and telephone her.'

'It's all right,' said Elizabeth. 'I don't expect she'll be worried. It's not as if it's dark yet – but all the same, I think I'd better go. Thank you very much for having me.'

'Thank you for coming,' said Mrs Dewar. 'It was really very good of you.'

Elizabeth was rather bewildered by this. Why was it good of her? No one had ever thanked her for *coming* before.

Paddy insisted on accompanying her as far as the bus stop and waiting with her until the bus arrived.

'It's my turn next, isn't it?' she said. 'I can come to you again, can't I? Can I come next Saturday? You come to me one Saturday, and I'll come to you the next. That's fair, isn't it?'

Elizabeth said that it was – she certainly couldn't see any objection to it. She and Jenny had always visited each other regularly, so there didn't seem any reason why she and Paddy shouldn't do the same. It wasn't as if she would be asking for chocolate pyramids and meringues every time. In future, they would just have ordinary things. Perhaps she might even ask if they could make up a sort of picnic and eat it by themselves in her bedroom. That would be fun.

It was just on half-past six when Elizabeth arrived home.

'You're late,' said her mother. 'I told you six o'clock. I told you to make sure—' She broke off. 'Good God in heaven! What on earth have you been up to?'

Following the direction of her mother's horrified gaze, Elizabeth glanced down at herself. The green stain on the front of her dress seemed mysteriously to have spread even further than when she had been scrubbing at it in Paddy's bathroom. The hem was hanging raggedly, her knee was all mottled and bloody where she had grazed it, her shoes still bore the evidence of having been immersed in scum-covered water. She hadn't realized until now quite how bad the damage was.

'What in heaven's name have you been doing?' said Mrs Muir.

'We've been exploring,' said Elizabeth. 'It wasn't Paddy's fault. *She* didn't make me. She gave me her socks to wear, because I stepped in some water and got wet.'

'So I can see,' said Mrs Muir. She said it rather grimly. 'I think you'd better go straight upstairs and have a bath . . . how anyone could let a child return home in such a state is simply beyond me to imagine.'

On Monday afternoon, when Elizabeth came home from school, Mrs Muir said: 'I bumped into Mrs Gower again today. In the supermarket. We went for a coffee together.' 'Oh, yes?' said Elizabeth, instinctively suspicious. What was coming now? Not *more* Sandra Gower?

'We had quite a long chat . . . it seems Sandra's only been at Gladeside a couple of terms. Apparently she hasn't settled down there too well. They're a bit worried about her.'

Elizabeth, drying her hands on the kitchen towel, concentrated on pushing her cuticles back, the way she had been taught. She didn't want to hear about Sandra Gower not settling down too well. She didn't want to hear about Sandra Gower, full stop. Sandra Gower was a nonentity.

'We both of us agreed that you ought to become friends,' said Mrs Muir. 'After all, you've got so much in common.'

In common? Her and Sandra Gower? Elizabeth glared, indignantly.

'Sandra used to go to a school very much like Lady Margaret. That was when they lived in London. When they moved out to Croydon they decided to try her at a state school, but it seems she hasn't found it at all easy. I believe some of the girls bully her rather, and that some of the boys are – well, rough, to say the very least.'

Elizabeth thought of Redmond, sticking his fingers up and swearing. Redmond was certainly rough. But you got used to him. He didn't mean anything by it. It was just his way.

'They're seriously thinking,' said Mrs Muir, 'of sending her somewhere else if the situation doesn't improve. The poor child simply isn't being given a fair chance.'

'It's her own fault,' said Elizabeth. 'It's because she's stupid. She doesn't do anything. She doesn't even *try*.'

'Well! That's not very charitable of you. She's probably shy – she probably needs someone to bring her out. That's where you could do a lot to help, if only you would. I've suggested to her mother that she comes round here on Saturday and has tea. That'll give you a chance to get to know each other better.'

'*What?*' Elizabeth sat up, poker-straight, in horror. 'But you *can't*! I've asked Paddy! It's her *turn!*'

There was a pause; then Mrs Muir said: 'As a matter of fact, I've been meaning to speak to you about Paddy . . . I don't mind you being friendly with her at school, of course, but I've come to the conclusion that I'd really rather you didn't see too much of her outside. I'm sure she means well, but—

'But *what?*' said Elizabeth.

'But exactly that! You've only known her three weeks and in that short time she's changed you completely. You're not at all the sort of girl you used to be. You've become rude, you've become defiant, you answer back – you don't get home when you're told to get home, you give things away without asking, you break things and don't tell us – you've become totally deceitful. I'm sorry, but I feel she's a thoroughly bad influence over you. I'm not saying it's her fault. She can't help the sort of background she comes from. It's just that it's not *our* sort of background, and I don't want you picking up her sort of habits. As for next Saturday, that's simply another example of what I've been talking about. Did you *ask* if you could invite her back to tea?'

'*No*,' said Elizabeth, 'but you *said*. When she was here before, you *said*—'

Mrs Muir tightened her lips.

'Elizabeth, I will not have that tone of voice. You know perfectly well that you should always check with me before you ask people round. I already postponed going to Granny and Grandpa. *Didn't* I? All because you didn't check first? Well, I'm not putting Sandra off. I've asked her to come, and she's coming. You'll just have to tell Paddy that you're very sorry but you made a mistake.'

'But I *can't*! I—'

'Elizabeth, please don't argue with me. If you will go round issuing invitations without first asking me whether it's all right, then you must take the consequences when it isn't. Now, hurry up and finish your tea, then go and get on with whatever prep you've got.'

'It isn't *prep*,' said Elizabeth. She snatched ungraciously at a slice of cake. 'It's *home*work.'

7

The last thought that Elizabeth had before falling asleep that night was, 'How ever am I going to tell Paddy?' It was also the very first thought that she had on waking up again next morning. It tormented her all through getting dressed, all through breakfast. Desperately, at the last minute, she said to her mother: 'Why couldn't Sandra come the Saturday *after*?' but Mrs Muir refused even to discuss it.

'We've already had all this out. Sandra is coming *this* Saturday and that is that.'

She knew that if she tried arguing it would only make matters worse. If there was one thing Mrs Muir wouldn't tolerate, it was what she called 'back chat'.

All the way up the road, Elizabeth rehearsed what she was going to say. 'My mother's gone and arranged something else,' or 'We've got to go over to Greenwich to see Uncle Clive,' or 'Daddy's taking us out in the car.' If she said that her mother had arranged something else, Paddy would want to know what; and if she said that her father was taking them out in the car, Paddy wouldn't understand why she couldn't go with them. She decided in the end to put the blame on Uncle Clive. She knew that the one excuse she couldn't make was the real one: she couldn't say that she was having to have Sandra Gower to tea instead of Paddy. That would be worse than mere disloyalty, it would be actual *treachery*.

Had she been brave, she would have broken the news immediately, as soon as they met, at their halfway point beside the statue of Queen Victoria. Unfortunately, in some matters Elizabeth was a coward – she really hated having to hurt people. The minute she saw her, Paddy gave an excited shout of 'I've just seen Miss Woods on the back of someone's *motor* bike!' and the temptation to talk about Miss Woods and to set other matters to one side was all too fatally easy. They talked about Miss Woods the whole of the way to school: by the time they reached the main gates, the news had still not been broken.

She made up her mind that she would do it before they went into assembly. The cloakroom wasn't any good, on account of being too crowded, and Paddy's peg not being anywhere near hers; but on their way up to the classroom she would quite *definitely* do it.

On their way up to the classroom, they were joined by Jo Ann. Jo Ann, as a rule, didn't have a great deal to say; just a quick 'Hi' and that was that. This morning, she wanted to talk.

'We're havin' a netball match against 1B next week. I'm gonna try out the teams on Friday. I got *you*—' she nodded at Paddy '—down as Centre. OK?'

'What about Elizabeth?' said Paddy.

'Dunno . . . might try her out as Goal Defence, if she likes.'

In normal circumstances, Elizabeth would have been rendered almost delirious by such an honour. To be tried out for a place on the class netball team

100

was beyond the very wildest of her expectations. (Not that she imagined for one moment that she would actually be chosen, but even just to be *considered* was enough for ecstasy.) Today, although naturally she was still pleased, she wished only that Jo Ann would go away and find someone else to talk to so that she could get the whole dreadful business over and done with.

'It's either her or Carmen,' said Jo Ann. 'I ain't decided yet.'

'You tried Carmen last time,' said Paddy. 'She wasn't any use.'

'Yeah, but she's bin practisin'.'

'So's Elizabeth,' said Paddy. 'Elizabeth's getting really good.'

That made her feel even worse than she had before. They reached the classroom and Jo Ann went off to speak to Julie Christmas. Elizabeth opened her mouth.

'Hang on a mo!' Paddy plonked down her Grants of Croydon bag. 'I just want to go and look at something.'

Before Elizabeth had a chance to speak, she was off and away across the room, to where Mrs Hyslop kept the Oxford English Dictionary.

'What is it?' said Elizabeth. 'I bet I can tell you.'

She prided herself on her spelling, and on her knowledge of what words meant, but Paddy wouldn't say what it was she was looking for; she said Elizabeth would have to wait until she had found out whether it really was a word 'or whether I've just made it up'. Seconds later, she slammed the dictionary shut and pranced jubilantly back across the room.

'It is! It's a South American fox, and it begins with a Z, and I'm going to use it when we play Scrabble on Saturday!'

Elizabeth felt a terrible sinking feeling; as if the pit of her stomach had just fallen away and all the contents had dropped out and were lying there in a big, heavy heap on whatever it was that was below them.

'Actually,' she said, miserably, 'I'd meant to tell you about Saturday . . . I made a mistake. I ought to have asked my mother first.'

'Why?' Paddy was staring at her, tense and strained. She had suddenly gone very pale beneath her freckles. 'What is it? What's wrong? Won't she let me come?'

'It's not that she won't let you, only—'

'*I*'m coming,' said Sandra Gower. 'Aren't I, Elizabeth?'

Elizabeth spun round, red-faced and indignant. Sandra Gower, with a stupid leer, was standing behind her.

'Her mother'th invited me,' she said.

'Honestly, I didn't know!' Elizabeth spun back again. 'I didn't know that she *had.*'

In a small, tight voice, Paddy said: 'Why can't I come as well? I was invited first.'

'No, you weren't,' said Sandra Gower.

'Yes, I *was*,' said Paddy. 'I was invited *weeks* ago. Weeks and *weeks* ago.'

'Well, you're not invited now, 'coth I am.'

'So why can't I come as well?' Paddy addressed herself, furiously, to Elizabeth. 'Why can *she* come and not *me*?'

Elizabeth didn't know how to answer. Sandra

102

Gower answered for her: ''Coth she doethn't *want* you. She wanth *me*.'

'It's not that!' said Elizabeth. 'It's—'

The bell, at this moment, rang for assembly. There was no opportunity for further talk. Mrs Hyslop was there, and they had to line up; and since they had to file into the assembly hall in strict order of height, it meant that Paddy was right down at the front of the line and Elizabeth right at the back, so that they couldn't even whisper.

As soon as they arrived back in the classroom, Mrs Hyslop started taking the register. Usually, either before or afterwards, she let them talk for a bit, but this morning she was obviously in a bad mood (like everyone else these days, thought Elizabeth, glumly) because the very minute she had finished she told them to take out their *Narrative Verses* and begin studying the poem on page twenty-four.

'And no gibble-gabble! Just get on with it.'

The poem on page twenty-four was *High Tide on the Coast of Lincolnshire,* which Elizabeth had already done at Lady Margaret. She didn't like it very much (she didn't like anything where people died) and, anyway, how could she concentrate on poetry with Paddy sitting white-faced and tight-lipped beside her, not communicating? At last, she could bear it no longer. Braving Mrs Hyslop's wrath, she leant across and whispered: 'I *didn't* know. *Honest.* Cross my heart, I *didn't.'* Paddy pushed her fringe out of her eyes.

'Why can't I come as well?'

There really wasn't any reason why Paddy couldn't come as well. No reason at all, except that

103

her mother didn't want her to. Elizabeth felt her cheeks glow with a give-away crimson; then Mrs Hyslop's voice cut across.

'Paddy Dewar, if you can't stop talking you can go and stand outside the door. Goodness knows, I've told you often enough.'

Elizabeth was aghast.

'Please, it wasn't Paddy,' she said, 'it was me.'

'Then if there's any more of it, *you* can go and stand outside the door. I will not have this constant stream of chit-chat and babble.'

For the rest of the class, there was silence. Mrs Hyslop's moods were proverbial. As a rule she was quite good natured, but every now and again she would have what was known as one of her breakouts, then woe betide anybody who was foolish enough to cross her. Rumour had it that on those mornings when she turned up in a temper it was because she and her husband had fought each other over the breakfast table. Mr Hyslop (according to rumour) threw his bacon to the floor and stamped on it; Mrs Hyslop flung saucepan lids. Elizabeth couldn't imagine Mrs Hyslop doing anything so undignified, but still she wasn't going to run the risk of being caught talking again. Outwardly, she concentrated on her narrative verse, the same as everyone else; inwardly, she wrestled with the problem of what she was to say to Paddy. You couldn't tell your best friend that your mother had decided she was a bad influence and mustn't be seen any more – in any case, she *was* going to see her. She couldn't believe that Mrs Muir had really meant what she said. It would be too unfair. Not even a mother could be as unfair as that.

The bell rang for the end of class. Mrs Hyslop, still in a mood, said: 'I want a fifty-word précis of the poem you've just read, and I want it for Friday. I will accept *no excuses* for work not done. Now, get your things packed up and hurry along, especially you girls. I've had complaints just recently from Miss Slade that you've been arriving late for her needlework classes. There's no earthly reason for it. You're not geriatrics. Pick your feet up and don't loiter and you can be there in bags of time.'

In spite of what Mrs Hyslop said, it was always a rush, trying to get from 1C at one end of the building to the domestic science block at the other before the next bell rang. It certainly didn't allow any time for talking, but fortunately Miss Slade wasn't too strict; she never minded if people sat and chatted as they sewed hems. She said that silence was unnatural, and that a bit of healthy hubbub helped you concentrate.

'*Honestly*—' under cover of the general buzz of conversation, Elizabeth edged her chair closer to Paddy's '—my mother's gone absolutely *potty*. She keeps meeting Mrs Gower in supermarkets, and they keep *talking* and drinking *coffee*, and that's why she's gone and invited her. Without even *asking* me. She goes on and on about me not asking *her*, then *she* goes and invites someone without even *bothering*—'

'*But why can't I come as well?*'

'Well, because – because Mrs Gower keeps telling her about how Sandra's not getting on here and how beastly everyone is and how people keep bullying her and—'

'Serve her right if they do. Soppy cow.'

'That's what I said,' said Elizabeth.

'So what are *you* s'posed to do?'

'I don't know . . . talk to her, or something. Bring her out; that's what *she* said.'

Paddy's eyes narrowed, accusingly.

'You're not going to be *friends* with her?'

'No, I'm not!' Elizabeth spoke vehemently. 'I'm jolly well not! I'm going to see her this once and that'll be bad enough. I'm not going to *keep* doing it.'

'So does that mean I can come *next* week?' said Paddy. Elizabeth must have hesitated very slightly. 'It will still be my turn!'

'Yes. I know it will.'

'So can I?'

'I'll have to ask her,' said Elizabeth. 'She's gone all funny just lately. I'll have to wait till she's in a good mood . . . I'll wait till Saturday's over. Then I'll ask her.'

Saturday turned out to be every bit as awful as she had known that it would (in spite of having chocolate pyramids *and* meringues *and* traffic lights for tea without her having had to ask for them). Sandra Gower was quite one of the stupidest people anyone had ever met. They played Scrabble again after tea and she couldn't spell even the simplest of words. Everyone had to keep cheating in order to help her, and all she did was laugh, as if it were something *clever* not to be able to remember 'i before e except after c' or that the plural of knife was spelt knives and not knifes. Before tea they had gone up to Elizabeth's bedroom, and instead of wanting to look at the books or the ornaments she had just wanted to talk about what her old school had been like and how much nicer it was than Gladeside.

'I *hate* Gladethide; don't you?'

'No,' said Elizabeth. 'I quite like it.'

'I don't know how you *can*. I think it'th *horrible*. People don't even *thpeak* prop'ly.'

Elizabeth wondered how she could say that, when she had to curl her tongue round a steel knitting needle and say Michael and Moses ten times a day.

'Wathn't *your* old thchool much nither? Weren't the *people* much nither?'

Elizabeth thought back to Jenny, and Christine Cottle, and Devi Shah – and then she thought of Paddy, and Sammy English, and John Diamond – and she wasn't so sure that they were. She didn't think now, if anyone were to ask her, that she would actually want to go back to Lady Margaret.

'They're all tho *rough*,' said Sandra. 'Honethtly, I *hate* it.'

When Sandra went home at six o'clock, Elizabeth was told by her mother to see her to the top of the road – 'It's only polite, with a guest.' She hadn't said that when Paddy had been a guest. (She hadn't used to say it with Jenny, either, but then one of Jenny's parents had always come to pick her up in the car.)

'Necktht week,' said Sandra happily, 'you're coming to uth.'

'Not next week,' said Elizabeth. 'I can't, next week.' *Or* the week after. *Or* the week after that.

'Yeth, you can,' said Sandra. 'You mother thaid you can. I athked her, and she thaid yeth.'

Elizabeth was indignant.

'When did you ask her?'

'Jutht now. Before we left. I athked her if you could come and she thaid you could.'

'Well, I can't,' said Elizabeth, ''cos Paddy's coming.'

'No, she ithn't,' said Sandra. 'Your mother won't let her.'

Elizabeth stared.

'What d'you mean, she won't let her?'

'I mean she won't let her. Not now. Not after what my mother told her.'

'What did your mother tell her?'

'About her father.'

'What about her father.'

Sandra paused, and cast a furtive glance over each of her shoulders.

'I'm not meant to know. But I heard them.'

'Heard *who*?'

'My mother and yourth. On the telephone. I heard them talking and I lithened.'

Yes, thought Elizabeth; that was just the mean, sneaking sort of thing that Sandra Gower *would* do.

'Listened to what?' she said, angrily.

'What they were thaying . . . I heard my mother eckthplaining why she wouldn't ever let me go to tea with Paddy Dewar.'

'Paddy wouldn't ever *ask* you to go to tea with her,' said Elizabeth.

'Oh, yeth, she would! She did! Latht term, she did. And my mother thaid I wathn't to go, tho there!'

Elizabeth looked at her, jealously.

'Why did she?'

'Becoth she'th common and she liv'th in a thlum and her father'th in prithon. *That*'th why.'

Elizabeth's heart missed a beat; she actually felt it miss one. She came to a standstill. What Sandra had said was a lie. She wouldn't believe it – she wasn't *going* to believe it.

'He's not in prison!' she said. 'He's away in America, making films!'

Even as she said it, she knew that it wasn't true. If Paddy's father were in America, making films, he would be making a lot of money. Everyone knew that poeple who made films made money. And people that made money didn't live in tiny little dolls' house cottages with leaking roofs and peeling wallpaper. They lived in big houses like Jenny did, with motor-cars and freezers. Paddy's mother hadn't even had a telephone, never mind a motor-car or freezer. Common sense should have told her . . . Paddy's father couldn't possibly be in America making films.

Her throat contracted. When she spoke, it was almost in a whisper.

'What did he do? To get put in—' She swallowed. She couldn't bring herself to say the word 'prison'. Obviously it must have been something terribly wicked. Nobody got sent to prison for no reason.

'I eckthpect he thtole,' said Sandra. 'That'th what they uthually do.'

Of course, stealing *was* bad; not a doubt of it. Stealing was very wicked indeed. Elizabeth tried hard to feel shocked, but all she could feel was desperately unhappy. She wished that Sandra had never told her. How dreadful to be Paddy, and have a father who stole! No wonder she made up

110

stories about him. Elizabeth would make up stories, if she had a father who did that. It had been dreadful enough when a policeman had come round one time, asking questions about a motor accident. She had been terrified for days afterwards, in case Mr Muir had done something wrong and was going to be taken away. Admittedly she had been only eight years old and too young to know any better, but in Paddy's case it had actually happened; Mr Dewar really *had* done something wrong; he really *had* been taken away.

'You're not to tell anyone,' said Sandra, ''coth I'm not thuppothed to know. It'th thuppothed to be a thecret. No one'th thuppothed to know. You've got to *thwear*.'

Elizabeth tossed her head.

'*I* don't give secrets away,' she said.

The subtlety of this was lost upon Sandra.

'You've thtill got to thwear. If you don't, I'll thay I didn't tell you. I'll thay it wathn't me.'

Elizabeth looked at her, contemptuously.

'I don't care what you say.'

'You would,' said Sandra, ''coth there'd be the motht awful futh. Thpecially if you went and told *her*.'

Told Paddy? She would sooner die. The very idea made her blush for shame.

They reached the top of the road.

'You thtill haven't thworn,' said Sandra.

'I haven't got a Bible,' said Elizabeth. 'You have to swear on Bibles.'

'Well, tho long ath you *promith*.'

There was a silence.

111

'All right, then,' said Sandra. 'I'll trutht you. Shall we go to thchool together on Monday?'

'I can't,' said Elizabeth. 'I go with Paddy.'

'But you can't *thtill* go with her. Not now that you *know*.'

'Of course I can!' shouted Elizabeth. '*I* don't care!'

She arrived back indoors to find Mrs Muir sorting embroidery silks at one end of the sitting room while Mr Muir watched television at the other.

'Well!' said Mrs Muir. 'That wasn't so very terrible, was it? All the fuss you made! And there she is, a perfectly pleasant, well-mannered girl . . . did she tell you, by the way, that Mrs Gower has asked you round there next Saturday?'

'Yes,' said Elizabeth.

'I think we really will have to try and get you a new dress for it. That one you wore the other day has been completely ruined. The stains won't come out, no matter how hard I—' She broke off. 'Now what's the matter?'

Elizabeth took a breath.

'If I've got to go to her place *next* Saturday,' she said, 'can Paddy come the Saturday after?'

There was a pause. Mrs Muir selected a skein of primrose yellow embroidery silk and thoughtfully held it up to the light.

'*Can* she?' said Elizabeth.

'The Saturday after? I wonder if this shade would suit you, or whether it would make you look sallow? Come here, and let me try . . . mm. Not very flattering. You need something stronger . . . the

Saturday after, I rather think we shall be going to Greenwich.'

'Well, can she come on the *Sun*day then?'

'Not on the Sunday, Elizabeth. No. I don't think so. We like a bit of peace and quiet on a Sunday.'

'Well, then, *when*? When *can* she come?'

'We'll discuss it later.' Mrs Muir closed the lid on her embroidery silks and stood up; a plain indication that the conversation was finished. 'Let's see how you get on with Sandra first. See how you feel when you've been round there next Saturday.'

'But I *know* how I'll feel. I'll feel exactly the same as I do now.'

'We shall see,' said Mrs Muir.

Tears filled Elizabeth's eyes.

'But what am I going to tell Paddy?'

'You tell her the truth: that you're going to have tea with Sandra. And that the week after that you're going to visit your aunt and uncle. Good gracious heavens! The child can't expect to monopolize the *whole* of your life.'

8

Monday morning, and the clock on the old town hall was already striking the half hour. Elizabeth heard it, but still her feet continued to drag. Punctuality, Miss Hutton had always said, was one of the prime virtues; but this morning she just couldn't have made her feet move any faster. Her shoes were lead weights, pulling her down into the pavement; her stomach felt as if it were full of bullet-hard rock cakes and soggy suet pudding.

She turned the corner, and there was the statue of Queen Victoria and there; by the statue, was Paddy, wearing her Lady Margaret beret with the teddy bear brooch and carrying her Grants of Croydon bag full of books. As soon as she saw Elizabeth, she came bounding forward, bright and eager, Tigger-like, beaming.

'Did you ask her? Is it all right? Can I come?'

It was the moment that Elizabeth had been dreading; it was the very worst moment in the whole of her life. Her mother had said tell the truth; but how could she? It *wasn't* the truth – not the real truth. The real truth was that Paddy's father was in prison and Mrs Muir didn't think she was a suitable person for Elizabeth to have for a friend.

The blood came rushing to her cheeks. She heard herself stammering – stumbling – blurting

114

out an incoherent jumble of disconnected words. 'My mother' – 'Mrs Gower' – 'got to go round there.'

'I've told her that I don't want to – she just won't listen. She says that I've *got* to. And next Saturday we're going to Greenwich, and when I asked her about Sunday she said she wanted peace and quiet, and—'

'You mean she won't let me come on Saturday *or* Sunday?'

'I've asked her,' said Elizabeth. 'I've asked her and *asked* her.'

'She won't let me come at *all*? Not *ever*?'

'She didn't say not ever. She just said wait and see. It's 'cos of the wheelbarrow and – and the flower beds and the fence and – and then me getting in late and messing my dress up and—'

'She doesn't like me,' said Paddy. 'She doesn't think I'm good enough for you.'

Elizabeth was horrified.

'No! It's not that! It's—'

'Yes, it is! She doesn't want you to be friends with me. Just because you live in a posh house and speak with a posh voice and went to a posh school . . . that's what it is!'

'*No*!' said Elizabeth. 'That's got nothing to *do* with it!'

'Then why doesn't she like me?'

'She *does* like you.'

'Then why won't she let me come?'

'Because – because I *told* you! She's in this mood! Because of the wheelbarrow and—'

'She doesn't like me,' said Paddy.

'She *does*!' Even to Elizabeth's ears, it lacked

115

conviction. 'It's just – well – I don't know! You oughtn't to have sworn.'

'I didn't swear!'

'Yes, you did! You said blast.'

'That's not swearing!'

'It *is* swearing.'

'No, it's not!'

'Yes, it *is*.'

'All right, then! It is! And I'll do it as often as I like . . . blast! blast! blast!'

Elizabeth pursed her lips.

'It's not clever to swear,' she said. 'People only swear when they can't think of anything else to say.'

'*I* can think of something else to say . . . I could say hell or bloody, or something even worse. If I wanted, I could say all *sorts* of things.'

'So could I,' said Elizabeth, 'but I wouldn't, because it doesn't sound nice.'

'Because it doesn't sound nice . . .' Paddy mimicked her, her voice pitched high. 'Who cares about *sounding* nice?'

'I do,' said Elizabeth.

She hated quarrelling with Paddy, but it really wasn't fair. She *had* sworn, and she must have known that she shouldn't. Anyone's mother would be angry.

'What would *your* mother say,' she said, 'if I came round and swore in your house?'

Paddy's face, which had been white, turned slowly pink.

'And then we *oughtn't* to have climbed over that fence,' said Elizabeth, ''cos it did say "Private". *And* "Trespassers will be Prosecuted". And if we hadn't climbed over, I wouldn't have torn my dress. It's all

116

very well you saying I've got loads of them, but I haven't got as many as all that, and I'd only had that one two months. She was ever so angry about it – *and* about the wheelbarrow. *And* about me getting home late.'

'You should've telephoned,' said Paddy. 'Like my mum said you should.'

'I couldn't, 'cos I didn't have enough money! I only had enough for my bus fare! If you'd got a telephone, the same as everybody else—'

She stopped. She hadn't meant to say that. It was a terrible thing to say. Paddy's face had gone from pink to scarlet.

'My mum would've *given* you the money . . . you'd only got to ask her for it. She'd have *given* it – Here!' She suddenly tore the Lady Margaret beret from her head and flung it to the ground. 'You can take back your rotten beret – and your rotten carrier bag!' Furiously, she upended the Grants of Croydon bag, dumped her books on the pavement, tossed the empty bag towards Elizabeth. '*I* don't want them! I wouldn't be seen *dead* with them!'

Snatching up her books, she turned, and set off at a run. Elizabeth, left alone, stood quite still for a few moments; then slowly she bent down and picked up the carrier bag, picked up the beret, put the beret inside the bag, the bag inside her satchel. She found that her hands were trembling, that her body had gone all weak and watery. It always upset her to fall out with people; but to fall out with *Paddy,* who was her best friend – or was she? Perhaps she wouldn't be, any more. Perhaps, after this, she wouldn't even want to talk. Elizabeth would talk; she hated disagreements far too much ever to bear grudges.

117

But then Elizabeth wasn't the one who had been hurt.

Slowly, and with foreboding, she made her way to school. Paddy must have kept up a fast trot, for she wasn't even a dot on the horizon, but as Elizabeth turned into Gladeside Avenue someone called her name from the opposite side of the road.

'Elithabeth! . . . *Elithabeth!*'

Her heart sank. Not Sandra Gower – not this morning. If she was to be seen going into school with *her*—

'I thought you were thuppothed to be meeting your friend?' Already she was crossing the road; making a beeline, straight for her. 'I thought you thaid you alwayth came with her?'

Elizabeth frowned, and swung her satchel. Maybe if she didn't say anything, Sandra would get bored and go away.

'Ithn't she coming?' said Sandra. Determinedly, she attached herself to Elizabeth's elbow. Elizabeth squirmed. 'Ith she ill? Ith it her mother? Thometimeth her mother gothe barmy and she hath to thtay away and look after her.'

'What do you mean?' She was betrayed into speech despite herself. 'What d'you mean, her mother goes barmy?'

'She gothe barmy. She jutht thtayth indoorth and crieth and won't do anything.'

'How do you know?' said Elizabeth.

'My mother knowth. She knowth thomeone who'th in the thocial thervitheth. I heard them talking about it.'

'You mean you *eaves*dropped,' said Elizabeth.

'I lithened,' said Sandra. 'My mother thaid that

119

she thought she ought to be put into care. In a childrenth home. She thaid—'

'I don't want to hear what she said!' said Elizabeth, angrily. 'You oughtn't to listen to other people's conversations.'

Sandra looked aggrieved.

'I thought you'd be int'rethted . . . theeing ath she'th your *friend*.'

They walked through the school gates and into the playground. Fat Spencer, eating something sticky out of a paper bag, came over to join them.

'Paddy's playing netball with Jo Ann,' she said.

'Tho she *ith* here,' said Sandra. 'I thought you thaid—'

Just at that moment, a netball came whizzing past: seconds later, and Jo Ann came whizzing after it. Normally she would have made some sign of having noticed Elizabeth; either shouting over her shoulder to her – 'Wanna join in, then?' – or actually lobbing the ball towards her by way of invitation. This morning she did neither. She didn't even look in her direction, even though she must have known perfectly well that she was there. Nobody could miss the great bulk of Fat Spencer.

Maybe that was it, thought Elizabeth, clutching at straws. Maybe Fat Spencer was the only thing that she had seen. After all, poor Fat was large enough to hide an army, never mind one skinny schoolgirl. Jo Ann simply hadn't noticed Elizabeth standing beside her, that was what it was.

She knew, as soon as the nine o'clock bell rang, that it wasn't. As she walked up the stairs towards 1C's classroom, in company with Sandra and Fat Spencer, who stuck like leeches, she heard Julie

120

Christmas's voice from somewhere behind. It was loud, and clear, and ringing.

'There goes Snobby, with her new friends . . .'

Someone giggled. Someone else, whose voice she didn't recognize – it might have been Redmond's – came jeering after her: 'Got a poker up your arse?'

Hot tears pricked Elizabeth's eyes. Her cheeks flared.

'That boy ith tho *common*,' said Sandra. 'If my mother could hear the thort of languace he utheth she'd let me go to another thchool right away.'

'So would mine,' said Fat.

'He ought to be in a *Borthtal*, or thomething.'

'Yes, he ought,' said Fat. 'Don't you think he ought, Elizabeth?'

Elizabeth didn't speak. She was too busy holding her head high to keep the tears in check. She wouldn't cry. She *wouldn't*. Some words that Miss Hutton had once told them came back to her: sticks and stones may break my bones, but names will never hurt me . . . She repeated it inside herself, over and over, as she went up the stairs.

'Sticks and stones may break my bones, but names will never hurt me . . . sticks and stones may break my bones—'

'Watch out!' A warning cry went up from someone stationed outside the classroom door. 'Watch yer language . . . 'ere comes Snobby!'

It wasn't true: names *did* hurt. They hurt every bit as much as sticks and stones.

'*Honethtly,*' said Sandra. 'Thome *people*.'

Redmond, roughly shoving past her, stuck his fingers in her face.

'You ought to be in a *Borthtal,*' shrieked Sandra.

Redmond's reply was so unspeakably rude that it made Paddy's 'blast' sound almost like baby talk. Elizabeth had never heard anyone use language as bad as Redmond's. Even so, her sympathies were all on his side. Everyone knew that Redmond had problems. It was a horrid thing to have told him, that he ought to be in a Borstal.

She walked to her desk under what seemed to be the hostile glare of the entire class, although in point of fact only about a dozen people were there.

'Know what her trouble is, don't ya?' said Jo Ann. 'Too high and bleedin' mighty, that's what her trouble is.'

'I'm surprised she can bear to sit in the same room,' said Julie Christmas.

'P'raps we oughta ask Mrs Hyslop for an oxygen tent for 'er?'

Elizabeth opened her desk and buried her head inside it. It's not fair, she thought. It's not *fair*. She knew that Paddy had been hurt, but it was mean of her to go spreading tales. Specially when they weren't true. She *wasn't* high and mighty: she *wasn't* a snob. It was her mother and Mrs Gower. They were the ones that were snobs.

Paddy didn't arrive until the last minute, when the bell was already ringing for assembly. She didn't look at Elizabeth; she simply marched up to her desk, took out her *Songs of Praise*, banged down the lid and quite deliberately turned her back. At break she went off with Julie Christmas and Janet Newman. Elizabeth found herself stuck, whether she liked it or not, with Sandra Gower: everyone else pointedly ignored her. Even John Diamond, who had always been polite and friendly, right from the very start, only said a stiff 'Thank you', accompanied by a curt nod of the head, as she retrieved a runaway football for him. Even Sammy English, who she had thought was quite beginning to like her, refused to speak, though he did seem a little shamefaced about it. Jo Ann and Julie Christmas were positively hostile, which meant that all the other girls were as well, because they always took the lead from them. Elizabeth had never thought the day would come when she would be glad of the company of Sandra Gower – not to mention poor Fat Spencer, lumbering like a great clumsy shadow behind them – but even Sandra Gower was better than no one. At least the rest of the school wouldn't realize that she had been made an outcast.

When she went back to the classroom after break, she found Paddy in the process of clearing out her desk, piling text books and exercise books on her chair, rounding up stray pens and pencils.

'What are you doing?' she said.

Without a word, Paddy scooped up her belongings and clutching them to her chest went stalking off across the room. In the far corner, just about as far away from Elizabeth as it was possible to get, was a spare seat; the girl who had sat there before having been transferred only last week to a special school for the educationally subnormal (Sandra said spitefully that that was where Redmond ought to go). Paddy now plonked herself and her possessions down into it with the air of one who intends taking up permanent residence; Elizabeth was left by herself, isolated and conspicuous, in the centre of the room.

As she undid her satchel to take out her fountain pen, a paralysing thought suddenly seized her . . . What about her paperweight? What about *Little Women*? Surely Paddy didn't think that she was going to *keep* them? Suppose she tried saying that Elizabeth had given them to her? Elizabeth couldn't prove that she hadn't. But it would be as good as *stealing*.

She opened her desk, and there they were. The paperweight and the book. Neatly placed one on top of the other, on top of her *Junior Arithmetic*. Hot waves of shame flooded her face. In her own mind, she had virtually accused Paddy of being a thief. She couldn't help wondering whether such a dreadful thought would ever have occurred to her if Sandra Gower hadn't told her about Mr Dewar being in prison . . . *I eckthpect he thtole. That'th what they uthually do . . .*

She *hated* Sandra Gower.

Later that day, when she took them for General Studies, Mrs Hyslop noticed that Paddy wasn't sitting where she usually sat. She said: 'Paddy Dewar, that's the third time this term you've changed places. Are you suffering from peregrinitis?'

There was a long silence, while Paddy, and everyone else, tried to decide whether she was or was not.

'That is a word I have just made up,' said Mrs Hyslop. 'It comes from the verb to peregrinate, which comes from the Latin word *peregrinus*. — Elizabeth, do you know what the Latin *peregrinus* means?'

'No,' said Elizabeth.

Someone tittered. Mrs Hyslop looked round, sharply.

124

'It means foreign. Thus, to peregrinate means to travel – ie, to go to foreign parts. Hence peregrinitis, meaning an excessive urge to move about. Why can't you keep still, like everyone else?'

Paddy didn't say anything. It was Jo Ann, aggressive, who said: 'Felt like a change of atmosphere, *din't* she?'

Mrs Hyslop raised an eyebrow.

'I wasn't aware that I was speaking to you, Jo Ann. Just mind your own business. Paddy has a tongue in her head, as I know to my cost. I just hope she doesn't think that because she's moved to the back of the room she can exercise it more fully than hitherto. Because if she does, I give her due warning . . . my hearing is very acute, and I can also lip read. All right?' She looked hard at Paddy. 'So long as that is understood. The first sign of talking, and I shall change *every*body round. Right! Let's get on with the lesson. Elizabeth, what have you brought for us?'

That evening, when Elizabeth went home, Sandra Gower attached herself. She tried to shake her off, but Sandra Gower was one of those people who wouldn't be shaken. She clung like a limpet, impervious to snubs.

'I would have walked home with you before, only you were alwayth with *her*. I'm glad you're not friendth with her any more. She'th not at all a nithe girl. My mother thayth she'th a thoroughly bad lot. She thayth she'll come to a thticky end one of thethe dayth if thomething ithn't done. She'th a liar, you know. She tellth the motht awful lieth. She told Janet Newman her mother wath a model. Can you imagine it? A *model*? And all she doth ith work in a fac'try! I mean, it'th pathetic, ithn't it? –

125

I thay, there'th a girl over there who theemth to be waving at you.'

The girl was Christine Cottle. She was on the other side of the High Street, in the familiar brown blazer and brown and gold beret of Lady Margaret, with a woman whom Elizabeth recognized from last term's Open Day as her mother.

'Do you know her?' said Sylvia.

'Yes,' said Elizabeth. She waved back. 'She goes to my old school.'

Christine Cottle passed on, with her mother, out of sight.

'I bet you wish you were thtill there,' said Sandra.

For the first time in weeks, she found that she did.

9

Every morning, now, Elizabeth found herself having to walk to school with Sandra Gower. There simply wasn't any getting away from her. She lay in wait at the end of the road, lurking behind someone's privet hedge, ready to step out as Elizabeth passed by. Elizabeth had tried leaving ten minutes early, and she had tried leaving ten minutes later, but it didn't make any difference: Sandra was always there.

Every morning when they arrived at school, Fat Spencer would be waiting for them in the playground, eating bars of chocolate or stuffing herself with crisps. Every break time they walked round together; an isolated trio, ignored by the rest of school society. Fat and Sandra spent their time grumbling about Redmond being coarse, or Jo Ann being rough, or Julie Christmas being a self-opinionated pig; Elizabeth spent hers trying her best not to notice what Paddy was doing, which wasn't easy because Paddy was always doing something. If she wasn't kicking a football about with some of the boys she would be playing netball with Jo Ann or leading a ball-grabbing expedition against another class. Paddy didn't belong to a gang, and she didn't have any special or particular friends, but everybody liked her. She never had any difficulty getting herself included.

Every dinner hour, Sandra went home and Elizabeth was left alone with Fat. She wished now that she hadn't made so much fuss about being allowed to stay on at school and eat in the canteen. She tried asking her mother if she could come home again, but Mrs Muir said no; she couldn't keep chopping and changing.

'You can come home again next term, if you want. For the rest of this term, you can stay as you are. I refuse to believe the food's as bad as all that.'

How could you explain that it wasn't the food, but the people? Everybody called her Snobby, now – everybody who counted. Paddy didn't talk to her, and John Diamond was too polite, but all the others had taken it up. She couldn't enter a room without somebody shouting it out . . . 'Watch it! Here comes Snobby!' Julie Christmas had even asked Mr Boyden, in all seeming innocence, what the French for a snob was.

'A *female* snob.'

'A female snob? Well—' Mr Boyden had considered it. 'I suppose you could call her *une prétentieuse.*'

Now, before every French class, she was met with a chorus of 'Ooh la la! Mademoiselle Prétentieuse!' Sammy English had a little song which he had learnt from his great-grandfather, who had fought in the first world war at a place called Mons, and when one day Mr Boyden asked if anyone knew any French songs, Sammy's hand shot up and he said 'Yes, sir!

128

Please sir! I do!' and had promptly proceeded to sing it:

Mademoiselle Prétentieuse
Parly voo?
Mademoiselle Prétentieuse
Parly voo?
Mademoiselle Prétentieuse
'Asn't bin kissed in *forty* years
Inky pinky *parly* voo.

Everyone (except Elizabeth and Sandra Gower) had collapsed with laughter. Even Fat had giggled – and then quickly put her hand over her mouth and looked ashamed. Even John Diamond had grinned. Mr Boyden, fortunately, hadn't known they were laughing at Elizabeth. He'd thought they were laughing because Sammy was singing a soldiers' song. But then, after joining in the merriment, he'd turned to Elizabeth and said, 'How about giving us a *real* French chanson, Elizabeth? I'm sure you must know one . . . how about *Au Clair de la Lune*? Suppose you sang that for us?' For days afterwards, people had kept breaking into high-pitched song every time she appeared: *Oh clair de la LOO-ny, mon ami peer-OH . . .*

Of course, she hadn't been included in the netball team for the match against 1A; she hadn't even been given the chance to try for it. Instead, a girl called Carmen Ojukwu had been chosen. Sandra Gower said that it wasn't fair. She said that Jo Ann had only chosen her because she was black.

'You're *ever* tho much better than she ith.'

To be honest, Elizabeth wasn't at all sure that she was; but anyway it hardly mattered any more. Jo Ann wouldn't choose her now if she were the best player in the class. Nobody would ever again choose her for anything. She knew that they wouldn't, because on Friday it had rained and they had had to stay indoors, in the assembly hall, and run races. Redmond and Sammy English, and Jo Ann and Carmen, had been told to pick teams; Elizabeth had been left to the very last. Even Fat Spencer had been picked before her. Nobody cared that she could run almost as well as a boy, and could hop-skip-and-jump faster than anyone else; they just didn't want her on their team. The very worst part had been the shame of it – standing there, as the numbers dwindled, and wondering, all the time, what Miss Woods must be thinking. Miss Woods, who usually took them for netball, *knew* that Elizabeth was good at running. She *knew* that Elizabeth would be a useful person to pick. When nobody did pick her she would put two and two together and work out that it must be because nobody liked her. Elizabeth couldn't bear Miss Woods knowing that. Miss Woods had played netball for England. She had dark curly hair and wore very short shorts, navy blue and pleated to look like a skirt, and her first name was Christine. Before, when she had been best friends with Paddy, Elizabeth had always done her best to shine in front of Miss Woods. She had gone out of her way to draw attention to herself. Now all she wanted to do was creep into a hole and not be seen.

'I think it'th awful,' said Sandra, 'the way they all gang up.'

'Who all gang up?' said Elizabeth. She was used, by now, to Sandra's constant grievances. She didn't always bother to listen.

'*Them.*' Sandra jerked her head towards the net-ball court, where 1C were playing their match against 1A. Carmen had just made a spectacular save and sent the ball hurtling up the court to Jo Ann. 'Jutht becoth they're black. If they want to come and live in thomeone elthe'th country, they ought at leatht to make an effort.'

'An effort to what?' said Elizabeth.

'Well . . . to be more like *uth.*'

Who'd want to be more like Sandra Gower? thought Elizabeth, sourly.

'They jutht don't try,' said Sandra. 'That'th what my mother thayth. She thayth they don't make any effort. They jutht gang up together. That'th why Carmen Ojukwu'th playing inthtead of you.'

'No, it isn't,' said Elizabeth. 'She's playing 'cos she's better than me.'

'Oh, Elizabeth, she's *not*,' said Fat.

'Yes, she is,' said Elizabeth.

'My mother thayth—'

Elizabeth put her fingers in her ears. She didn't want to hear any more of what Sandra Gower's mother said. She hated Sandra Gower's mother. She had known that she hated her even before she had gone round there for tea, but going round for tea had only confirmed it. She was a big, self-important, powdery woman, who kept saying things like, 'And how do *you* find Gladeside, Elizabeth? It must be *very* different from Lady Margaret . . . how do you find the other pupils? Don't you find them rather rough and ready? After Lady Margaret?' Elizabeth had refused to be drawn. She had known perfectly well what Mrs Gower wanted her to say, but she had stood

132

firm and wouldn't say it. Sandra had said it for her.

'They're being abtholutely *beathtly* to Elithabeth, jutht becoth she'th not friendth with that girl any more. Aren't they, Elithabeth?'

'Not particularly,' said Elizabeth. They *were* being beastly, but wild horses wouldn't have dragged it out of her. Not in front of Mrs Gower, whose fault it all was. She might have felt she scored a victory.

One morning when Sandra jumped out from behind her privet hedge her face wore an expression of barely suppressed excitement mixed with an almost gloating triumph. Taking Elizabeth's arm, she said: 'I've got thomething to tell you . . . but I'm not going to tell you what it ith till Pat'th here, tho you'll jutht have to wait.'

Elizabeth didn't mind waiting. She didn't expect it was anything that was likely to be of interest to her.

She was wrong. For once, Sandra really did have something to tell.

'Mummy'th agreed that I can go to Clare Court . . . I'm going to thtart necktht term − it'th all arranged! And becoth there'th only three weekth of thith term to go, she thayth I can leave Gladethide *now*. She'th coming to tell Mr Farmer today. She'th going to tell him how unhappy I've been, and how beathtly everyone ith, and how she doethn't want me to have to put up with it any more . . . ithn't it thuper?'

Fat looked doubtful; but loyally she said: 'Gosh, yes. Super.'

Elizabeth didn't say anything. The news had

come as a shock. She had grown so accustomed to Sandra's whining about how awful Gladeside was, and how awful all the people were, that she had long since ceased to attach any meaning to it. She had never for one moment thought that Sandra would really manage to talk her mother into letting her leave. A sort of panic swept over her. Ghastly though Sandra was, she was at least *some*one. Fat obviously felt the same (or perhaps she didn't think that Sandra *was* ghastly).

'I wish *I* could go to Clare Court,' she said.

'Why don't you athk them?' said Sandra. 'Why don't you *both* athk them? Then we could all of uth go — it'd be ever thuch fun! And it'th *heapth* better than Gladethide. *Honethtly*.' She turned to Elizabeth. 'It'th jutht like the thchool you uthed to go to before.'

Elizabeth's thoughts went winging back to Lady Margaret. The neat rows of girls in their brown and their gold . . . Miss Hutton teaching *mensa,* a table, *agricola,* a farmer . . . Miss Lowman, with her dark hair that pulled back into a bun and her gold-rimmed spectacles that hung on a chain . . . her heart swelled. Sandra was right: it *was* heaps better than Gladeside. Gladeside was a lousy, rotten, horrible place. Mr Farmer hadn't said so much as one single word to her since the day she had arrived; at Lady Margaret, Miss Lowman had spoken to *every* girl at *least* once a week. She had made a point of it. And Mrs Case, in the office, had known everybody by name and all about their families. Miss George, at Gladeside, probably wouldn't even recognize you in the street, never mind know your name. Never *mind* know about your family. It was ridiculous, having a school this size. It was ridiculous having boys. Boys were hateful and rough, and Redmond *ought* to be in a Borstal. And it was *horrid* of Sammy English to have turned against her, just because everyone else had. After all the trouble she'd gone to, helping him with his commas and his full stops, and now all he could do was stand up and sing beastly songs about her. And as for Julie Christmas and Jo *Ann*—

Tears came to her eyes. She blinked them away.

'All right,' she said. 'I'll ask them.'

'Yes,' said Fat. 'So will I.'

At tea that night, Elizabeth said: 'Sandra's not coming back to school any more. She's going to another one next term.'

'Yes, I know,' said Mrs Muir. 'Her mother rang me up this morning. Apparently they've decided the poor child just can't take any more of it.'

Any more of what? thought Elizabeth. Sandra hadn't been called Snobby and had beastly songs sung about her.

'It's a thousand pities you couldn't have made friends earlier. You might have been able to give her a bit more confidence. She just wasn't able to make the transition.'

Elizabeth wasn't sure what transition meant. Normally she would have asked. Today she didn't bother: there were more important matters at stake.

'She's going to a place called Clare Court,' she said.

'That's right. It's a little private school up near the Water Tower. They think she'll probably do better there.'

'Can *I* go there?' said Elizabeth.

'You?' Her mother looked at her in surprise. 'What do you want to go there for? I thought you were quite happy where you are.'

'No,' said Elizabeth.

'*No?*'

'I mean . . . not without Sandra.' She wasn't telling even her mother the real reason. She couldn't. It was too shameful. To *admit* to someone that they called you Snobby and sang songs about you.

'I didn't think you cared all that much about Sandra. That's what you've always led me to believe.'

'You said I'd got to be friends with her.'

'Yes. Well—' Just for a moment, Mrs Muir seemed at a loss. Then she rallied. 'No one can *make* people be friends with each other. I just thought that it would have been nice if you could. But perhaps in the circumstances it's just as well it didn't work out. I had no idea they were seriously thinking of taking her away. Not immediately.'

'She's already left,' said Elizabeth. 'She's not coming back.'

'No. I must say I thought that was a bit extreme. Unless they were actually bullying her—' Mrs Muir looked at Elizabeth. 'They weren't . . . threatening her, or anything?'

'They just didn't like her,' said Elizabeth. 'Nobody likes her.'

'Then why are you bothered that she's leaving?'

'Because *I* want to leave! I want to go to a school like Lady Margaret!'

'Oh, now, Elizabeth! We've already had all this out. You know we agreed—'

'*I* didn't agree! I wasn't even *asked*!'

'No, well, Daddy and I agreed. Because we're the people responsible. We discussed it very, very carefully, I promise you. And we both came to the conclusion that it would be far better for you—'

'Yes! I know all that! But it *isn't*. You were the one that said I wasn't behaving like I used to . . . well, it's this school! It's this school that's doing it to me!'

'Nonsense! There's nothing wrong with Gladeside. It has an excellent reputation. It was just that child you were seeing such a lot of . . . Paddy, or whatever her name was. She wasn't good for you.'

'It wasn't Paddy, it's the *school*. It's the *school* that's not good for me. That's why I want to leave!'

'Well, you can't,' said Mrs Muir. 'So that's that.'

'But they don't do *Latin*,' said Elizabeth, growing desperate.

'I'm not quite sure why you should have any need of Latin, but if it still bothers you when you're older I daresay we might be able to arrange for private tuition.'

'But I want to do it *now*, not when I'm older!'

'As a matter of fact, they probably don't do it at Clare Court, either. It's only a very tiny place. You'd need to go to the High School, or—'

'Then why can't I? *I* don't mind where I go, so long as it's not Gladeside! Why *can't* I go to the High School?'

'Purely and simply, because we can't afford it,' said Mrs Muir. 'There, now!' There was a silence. 'Does that satisfy you?'

'You could afford Lady Margaret,' said Elizabeth.

137

'That was when Daddy still had his old job. Things have changed since then . . . you must have noticed?'

Yes; of course she had noticed. A smaller house, a smaller car . . . she wasn't stupid. It was just that nobody had told her.

She spoke in a small voice.

'So even if we'd stayed in Caterham, I'd still have had to leave?'

'I'm afraid so,' said Mrs Muir. 'That was part of the reason we moved away . . . we thought it would make it easier for you. A totally fresh start. A different school, a different place—'

Elizabeth didn't say anything. She was too busy thinking, *so Jenny was right* . . .

She felt betrayed. *She* hadn't known; but Jenny had. Jenny had known all along. Why couldn't they have told her? Why couldn't they *ever* tell her *any*thing?

10

Fat's parents had said no, just as Elizabeth's had. On the whole, Elizabeth was relieved — she supposed that even Fat's great moon-shaped presence was better than total isolation. She kept reminding herself that Fat, after all, couldn't *help* being fat: she didn't eat all the time because she was greedy, but because she was unhappy. Everyone knew that fat people were unhappy. The trouble was that knowing it didn't necessarily make it any easier to like her. Even apart from her fatness, there were times when she could really be a very trying sort of person.

One Friday morning, before starting her English class, Mrs Hyslop announced that a girl from 1B called Dilys Harper had had a sum of money stolen from her coat pocket. She had left it there that morning, because she had been late for assembly and in a hurry, and by the time that she had remembered it and gone back again, about twenty minutes later, it had disappeared. Mrs Hyslop wanted to know if anyone from 1C could tell her anything about it. Needless to say, no one could.

'Well, if anybody suddenly remembers something,' said Mrs Hyslop, 'don't be afraid to come and tell me.'

Later on, during break, speaking through a

mouthful of cream bun, Fat said: 'Paddy Dewar was late for assembly this morning . . . she didn't get here till after prayers.'

Elizabeth came to a halt. What was Fat trying to say? That *Paddy* had taken Dilys Harper's money? She thought back to assembly that morning. She remembered them all singing 'The Church's One Foundation', she remembered Mr Farmer reading out a notice about collecting silver paper for guide dogs, she remembered – she remembered seeing Paddy's small figure worming its way in through one of the side doors, doing its best to slip unobtrusively into its place at the front of the hall. She turned, accusing, to Fat.

'Paddy wouldn't take money,' she said.

'She might,' said Fat. 'Anyone might, if it was there. If they knew about it . . . like your paper-weight. She knows about that.'

'So does everyone else,' said Elizabeth.

'No, they don't.' Fat was obviously in one of her argumentative moods. 'Not everyone knows that it's still here. Some people think you've taken it back home.'

Elizabeth bit her lip. There wasn't any answer to that. The truth of the matter was, she *ought* to have taken it back home. She knew that she ought. She hadn't quite liked to while Paddy had still had it in her possession, in case it made Paddy think she didn't trust her; and then afterwards, when there hadn't been any reason for keeping it any more, since everyone had already seen it and the novelty had long since worn off, she just hadn't been able to bring herself to remove it. It had become like a talisman – like a good luck charm. So long as it stayed there, there was just a chance that she and Paddy might one day be friends again. Take it away, and the chance would be gone. She knew that it was silly and superstitious, like not walking under ladders and not stepping on the cracks in paving stones, and that really and truly it didn't make the slightest bit of difference. She knew that it was only *sensible* to take the paperweight home – but how could she, when it would mean the end of all hope?

'Imagine if it got *stolen*,' said Fat.

Elizabeth shifted, uncomfortably.

'Who'd want to steal a paperweight?'

'Some people would steal anything,' said Fat. 'I mean, it's valuable, isn't it? It was your *grand*mother's.'

Great-grandmother's – it had been in the family over one hundred years. Maybe she *ought* to be sensible and take it back. After all, it didn't look as if Paddy was ever even going to speak to her again, let alone be friends.

Fat, obviously sensing that she had touched a weak spot, became daring.

'Paddy Dewar does steal things . . . I know she does, 'cos I've seen her. Once when we went up to London with Mr Ward she found a whole five pound note in the street and she kept it. She said it was hers and she was going to spend it. And when we told Mr Ward, he just laughed. He didn't tell her to go to the police station or anything. He just said finder's keepers and what was she going to spend it on, so then she went and bought some sweets and he ate one, and she never even offered them to me or Sandra. She's ever so mean. She'd go and steal your paperweight just to spite you. Just

141

because you're not friends with her any more. It's just the sort of thing she'd do. Sandra's mother—'

A wave of irritation swept over Elizabeth.

'I don't want to hear about Sandra's mother! I *hate* Sandra's mother – and I hate *you*, as well, when you make horrid insinuations! Paddy wouldn't *ever* steal my paperweight. She wouldn't ever steal *anything*. Finding money in the street's not stealing!'

'Elizabeth, it *is*,' said Fat.

'No, it's not! You could be locked up for saying things like that. Going round saying things that aren't true . . . you could be put into *prison* for it.' Even as she spoke, she remembered Paddy's father. *I eckthpect he thtole thingth* . . . She turned on Fat, angrily. 'You're wicked – you're *evil*! How would you like it if someone went round telling people that you stole?'

Fat's jaw had dropped open. She stared at Elizabeth, pop-eyed.

'But, Elizabeth, I only—'

'You said she stole things! You said you'd seen her! You were trying to make out that it was her that took that money!'

Fat rallied slightly.

'Well, but it could have been. She *was* late for assembly, and it's funny it was the very same morning, and I've just remembered something else.' Her pale, globular face, all covered in cream from its cream bun, glistened triumphantly. 'Yesterday dinner time she went out and bought chips. She was offering them to people.'

'So what?' said Elizabeth, fiercely. 'What if she did?'

'So she never does, as a rule. She never buys

anything. She never has any money. So where did she get it from if she hasn't been stealing it? I mean, she must have got it from *some*where, and Dilys isn't the only person to have lost money. Lots of people have. Laurel Piper in Class 3 had a one pound note pinched. *I* think we ought to tell Mrs Hyslop. After all, she did ask.'

'If you tell Mrs Hyslop,' said Elizabeth, 'I won't ever speak to you again . . . I won't! I mean it! I won't *ever*.'

'But Elizabeth, it's our duty,' said Fat.

'It isn't our duty! If people are stupid enough to leave great sums of money lying around in their coat pockets then they jolly well *deserve* to have them pinched.'

'But Mrs Hyslop *said*.'

'She didn't say we had to tell tales!'

'She asked us if we knew anything.' Fat could be maddeningly obstinate when she chose. 'That means that she wanted us to tell her. She wanted us to *say*.'

'All right, then! You *go* and say – you *go* and tell tales! Just don't come near me again, that's all!'

'But, Elizabeth, she *said*—'

'I don't care what she said! If you tell her, I don't want anything more to do with you!'

'You're only saying that because it's Paddy Dewar. You don't care that she's a thief and that she tells lies. You'd like to be friends with her again, wouldn't you?' Fat spoke jealously. 'You'd rather be friends with her than with me.'

'Yes,' said Elizabeth. 'I would. I should think anyone in their right senses would. You're horrible – you're *ugly*. You're like a great fat *slug*.'

143

Under its covering of cream, Fat's face had turned waxy yellow. The big blubber lips were quivering, the fishy eyes, protuberant behind thick-lensed spectacles, started in terror from their sockets.

'You do nothing but *eat*,' said Elizabeth. 'Eat and tell tales . . . you make me feel *sick*.'

She turned, and marched into school. Fat could follow, if she wanted. She couldn't stop her *following*.

The first class after break was Physics, with Miss McMaster. Of late, Elizabeth had been sitting with Fat on the back bench. Today, deliberately, she took a seat at the front. It was the last one there was, so that Fat couldn't come and sit next to her even if she wished. It would serve her right, thought Elizabeth, for saying hateful things about Paddy.

The week before, they had done an experiment to find the density of a zinc cylinder; this week, they were going to do one to discover what happened to hot air when it was heated. Miss McMaster divided them into groups, two to a bench, and each group was given its own apparatus to set up. The apparatus for the hot air experiment consisted of a glass-fronted box, two glass chimneys, a candle and a length of cord. Elizabeth's group set busily to work, but had barely inserted the glass chimneys into the holes at the top of the box before there came a shrill cry from the back of the room: 'Please, miss, Fat Spencer's eaten our candle!'

Somebody giggled. Several people groaned. Somebody else said: 'Not *again*?' Miss McMaster set down her glass chimneys and went hurrying up the gangway.

'What in the name of heaven—'

'She's gone and *eaten* it.'

'Our *candle*—'

'Eaten your candle?' Miss McMaster had been new that term. She didn't know about Fat's eating habits. She stared, nonplussed. Fat stared back, glassy-eyed, with a silly, self-satisfied grin on her face. Someone called out: 'She's always doing it, miss.' Elizabeth wondered whether she ought to feel guilty, and decided that she didn't; it wasn't *her* fault if Fat resorted to eating candles in moments of stress.

'She's bloody mad,' said Jo Ann. 'Just does it to get attention.'

'Stupid fat cow.' That was Julie Christmas. 'Makes herself ill with it.'

'Bloody well deserves to . . . eating bloody candles.'

'All right! All right!' Miss McMaster held up a hand. 'That's quite enough. – Dawn, take Pat along to the nurse and tell her what she's done. Then come straight back. The rest of you, get on with your work.'

Dawn returned, a few minutes later.

'What did the nurse say?' said Miss McMaster.

'She's got to stay lying down till dinner time.'

'Does she think she'll be all right?'

'She's always all right,' said Jo Ann. 'She just sicks it all up. She's bloody *mad*.'

They didn't see Fat again for the rest of the morning. At dinner time, alone, Elizabeth ate sausages and lumpy mash in the canteen. Afterwards, in the playground, she saw Paddy, handing round a bag of sweets to Jo Ann and Carmen and a group of others. It looked like quite a large bag. The thought came to her, unbidden; how awful if Paddy really *had* been taking money. What Fat had said about her not usually having any was quite true. Elizabeth knew that it was, because once when she'd suggested they go halves on a bar of chocolate, Paddy had said that she only had her dinner money on her. It was all she ever brought. She didn't even bring enough for a bus fare, or ten pence for the telephone. Now she was offering sweets to practically everybody in the playground.

Paddy looked up, and their eyes met. Elizabeth flushed. Hurriedly, she turned away – and almost bumped headlong into Miss Woods. That embarrassed her even more. Miss Woods was obviously on playground duty. Whatever happened, she mustn't see Elizabeth walking round all by herself. There must be somebody, somewhere—

Over in the far corner, some girls from 1A were playing with a length of old clothes line, using it as a skipping rope. Skipping was regarded as too childish for words in 1C. Jo Ann had declared that it was kids' stuff, since which time skipping ropes had been looked upon with contempt and brought to school at one's peril. Elizabeth didn't care; *she* still enjoyed it. They had done a lot of skipping at Lady Margaret. She and Jenny had been champions. She bet she could outskip anybody in 1A.

Made bold by desperation (she *couldn't* be seen spending the whole dinner break by herself) she approached the group. They were playing Keep the Kettle Boiling, running one after another into the rope and out again. Perhaps if she were simply to tag on at the end . . .

One of the girls turning the rope suddenly glanced up and saw her. Her gaze was not particularly encouraging, but neither, on the other hand, was it actively hostile. Elizabeth smiled at her, hopefully. The girl shifted a wodge of chewing gum from her right cheek to her left.

''Ullo, Snobby . . . what d'you want?'

One of the other girls, running round again to take her place in the line, gave Elizabeth a little shove.

'Where's your fat friend? All clogged up with candle grease?'

The girl following behind *her* stuck her face close to Elizabeth's.

'Why don't you get lost? *Snobby.*'

'What's she doing 'ere?'

'Tell 'er to bugger off!'

'Yeah, go on . . . 'oppit! *We* don't want yer!'

Elizabeth didn't stay to argue. Trembling, she turned and went. She found that she was shaking all over, her legs gone to jelly, just like on the day that she had quarrelled with Paddy. But she must keep walking. It was important that she kept walking. Rapidly up one side of the playground she trod; down again on the other. Past the bicycle sheds, past the main gates – past the entrance to the cloakrooms, on towards the science block – it didn't matter *where* she walked, so long as she walked purposefully, so that if Miss Woods should happen to see her she wouldn't realize that she was all by herself. She would think she was on her way somewhere. Going to a music lesson, going to a netball practice. Going *some*where.

Except that if Miss Woods saw her passing the

main gates for the second time, she would know perfectly well that she wasn't going anywhere at all, but was simply moving in circles.

She must find somewhere to *go*.

The entrance to the cloakrooms was coming up again. She would go down to the cloakrooms and sit on the hot-water pipes.

It was against school rules to sit on the hot-water pipes – it was against school rules even to sit in the cloakrooms. You were supposed to stay outside, getting the fresh air. At least, that was what Mrs Hyslop had said when some of 1C had complained.

'You shouldn't want to stuff about indoors . . . you should be outside, getting the fresh air.'

Reluctantly, Elizabeth turned her back on the cloakrooms and wandered instead up to the main corridor. There was at least another fifteen minutes to go until the bell rang – and even when it did, it was still Friday afternoon. She had come to dread Friday afternoons. Friday afternoons meant Improvisation with Miss Crompton, followed by a double period of PE. Improvisation was all right; it was PE which had become the nightmare. She prayed all week long, 'Please, God, don't make it rain on Friday . . . please, God, not on Friday . . .' She knew that it was silly and superstitious – just as silly and superstitious as not taking her paperweight home, because even if there was a God she didn't see why He should listen to *her* petty little prayers. After all, who was Elizabeth Muir to God? She wasn't anyone. Still she went on praying to Him. She prayed now, as she looked out of the windows. Please, God, please . . . don't make it rain . . . not on a Friday . . . The sky was ominously grey and

148

overcast. But nothing as yet had actually happened. With any luck—

She reached out a hand to touch a piece of wood, but couldn't find any. Everything was plastic, or metal. Where was there some wood? There must be some wood *some*where.

Her desk. That was wood. You weren't really meant to go back to the classroom during break times, but it was important she find some wood to touch. In any case, she couldn't go out to the playground again. Not with Miss Woods there. She *couldn't*.

As she reached the end of the corridor and turned left, towards the classrooms, she crashed into Paddy, coming the opposite way. They both recoiled, as if the other were a wild animal that might suddenly go mad and bite. There was an awkward pause, then:

'Have you had an accident?' said Elizabeth.

Paddy was holding up one finger, wrapped in a blood-stained handkerchief. She hid it hastily – almost guiltily – behind her back.

'Cut myself.'

'Oh.'

Another pause.

'Want a sweet?' said Paddy.

She pulled a crumpled bag of toffees from her pocket. They were some of Elizabeth's favourites – soft cream caramel covered in chocolate. She took one, awkwardly.

'Thank you,' she said.

''Sall right,' said Paddy. She hesitated, seemed on the point of saying something else, changed her mind and stuffed the toffees back again into her pocket. 'Got to go and get a bit of sticking plaster. Stop it bleeding.'

Paddy disappeared, in the direction of the sick room. Elizabeth walked on, down the corridor. Her heart felt like a big, air-filled balloon. Her feet were on springs. They had talked . . . they had actually *talked*! For the first time in almost three weeks. The first time since that dreadful morning by the statue of Queen Victoria, when Paddy had torn off her Lady Margaret beret and thrown her Grants of Croydon bag to the ground. And now she had offered her a toffee . . . The air-filled balloon that was Elizabeth's heart expanded almost to bursting point. She had *known* that it was right not to take the paperweight home.

She remembered that she had been on her way to touch wood. She supposed she had better go and do it. After all, Paddy's offering her a toffee wasn't going to change anything. Not immediately. They would still call her Snobby; she would still be left until last if they had to run races.

The classroom was empty. Closing her eyes, Elizabeth laid both hands flat on the top of her desk lid and fervently gabbled off her prayer: 'Please, God, don't make it rain . . . not on a Friday . . . let it be netball! Let it not be races! Please, God . . .'

She became aware that her feet were treading on something hard and crunchy. She opened her eyes, and looking down to see what it was found that the floor by her desk was covered in dozens of little white specks, like tiny pieces of gravel. Curious, she bent to examine them: they still looked like tiny pieces of gravel. The floor, she noticed, was glistening rather oddly, as if some sort of sticky substance had been spilt over it. She stretched out a hand to touch it – and made the unwelcome discovery that there was glass there as well as gravel.

'Ow!' She straightened up, sucking a finger. Where was it from, all this glass? What were they, all these little pieces of gravel?

My paperweight, she thought.

My *PAPERWEIGHT*.

She flung back the lid of her desk, and there it was. The tiny figures were still intact – the boy with his knickerbockers and his muffler, the girl in her red cloak and tartan beret – the little black dog still pranced at their side, the robin still sang on the branch of his tree, but the whole of their beautiful glass-enclosed world had been smashed, broken into a thousand fragments, the roof blown to smithereens over their heads.

Just at first, she felt shock, and a kind of numbness. Who would do such a thing? Who would *do* such a thing?

And then came the realization . . . she knew who had done it, didn't she? She had almost seen her do it. A few seconds earlier, and she would have caught her in the act.

Hot tears pricked at Elizabeth's eyes. Self-pity welled inside her. Welled and swelled until she thought that she would burst with it. Her throat was aching, a band stretched tight across her chest. To have offered her a *toffee*—

The bell rang for afternoon class. She slammed down her desk lid, snatched up her satchel, and ran. The rest of the school were all coming the other way. Elizabeth blundered through them, scarcely

151

seeing. Down in the cloakroom, she tore her coat from its peg, stumbled back with it up the steps, out across the playground and away through the main gates.

Dimly, she heard a voice (Miss Woods'?) calling after her: 'Elizabeth! Where are you going?'

Engulfed in tears, she ran blindly on. Miss Woods's voice echoed pleadingly in her wake: 'Elizabeth! Elizabeth! Come back!'

It was as she reached the end of Gladeside Avenue that the first drops of rain began to fall.

11

If there had been any conscious thought at all in Elizabeth's head as she ran through the main gates, it had been, 'Now they'll *have* to let me go to another school . . . they can't send me back after *this*.'

To her horror, even before she had finished sobbing out her story, Mrs Muir was on the telephone to Mr Farmer demanding an immediate appointment.

'I feel it shouldn't be allowed to hang fire . . . no. Precisely. So if you could . . . thank you so much! We'll be round straight away.' She replaced the receiver. 'Right! Let's go and get all this sorted out.'

'I haven't got to come *with* you?'

'Of course you must come with me! Mr Farmer's going to want to talk to you – get to the bottom of things. Find out who's responsible. Come on, now! Be brave! Dry your eyes and let's get off. The sooner it's over, the better.'

Mr Farmer listened with grave attention as Mrs Muir relayed the story.

'Calling her names . . . bullying her . . . making her life a misery. Now, to cap it all, someone has quite deliberately gone and smashed a rather valuable paperweight. I know she ought not to have brought the paperweight to school in the first place, but that, for the moment, is beside the point. The point is that there is obviously some child in the form who is a delinquent. I understand that only this morning there was a sum of money stolen from someone's coat pocket—'

Mr Farmer held up a hand.

'I have to stop you there, Mrs Muir. We *thought* there had been a sum of money stolen. It now seems that Dilys made a mistake . . . when she went home for lunch she discovered that the money was still there, on the kitchen table. In her hurry, she'd forgotten to take it. So you see there can be no question of accusing anyone of both crimes – if indeed, the breaking of the paperweight *was* a crime.' He turned, questioningly, to Elizabeth, sitting watery-eyed on the edge of a chair. 'How can you be so certain that it wasn't an accident?'

Elizabeth stayed silent. She *knew* that it hadn't been an accident. Paddy had broken it on purpose, in order to hurt her.

'Where was the paperweight?' said Mr Farmer. 'On top of your desk? Inside the desk? Inside the desk. Well, then, isn't it possible that someone took it out to have a look at it, and then was too scared to own up when it got broken?'

Mrs Muir said sharply: 'Surely pupils have no right to go taking things out of other people's desks?'

'Children will be children, Mrs Muir. As you yourself said, Elizabeth ought not to have brought such a valuable object to school with her in the first place. It really was a very silly thing to do. However, what I'm more interested in at this moment is discovering why she thinks it wasn't an accident. You still haven't told me, Elizabeth. Are you saying that you honestly believe someone took

155

the paperweight out of your desk and deliberately smashed it?'

Elizabeth bit her lip and didn't say anything.

'You honestly do believe,' said Mr Farmer, 'that there is someone in your class who would be capable of such a thing.'

'After all the bullying and name calling,' said Mrs Muir, 'it seems a not unreasonable conclusion.'

'Hm.' Mr Farmer brought the tips of his stubby fingers together and pondered Elizabeth over the top of them. 'What form, exactly, does this bullying take, Elizabeth?'

Elizabeth was alarmed: *she* hadn't said anything about bullying. Nobody had bullied her. Only called her names.

'Has anybody threatened you? Used violence towards you? Broken any of your things – apart from the paperweight, that is?'

Elizabeth swallowed, and shook her head.

'Well, then . . . is there anybody you're frightened of? You're not used to being at school with boys, are you? Have any of the boys frightened you?'

'No,' said Elizabeth.

'What about that rough boy?' said Mrs Muir. 'The one that uses all the language?'

'Redmond doesn't frighten me,' said Elizabeth. He had at first, it was true, but she was used to him by now. Redmond made a lot of noise, but he never actually did anything.

'So if nobody frightens you,' said Mr Farmer, 'what do they do to you? Just call you names?'

Elizabeth nodded.

'As if that's not enough!' Mrs Muir sounded

indignant. 'Calling people names can be quite sufficient intimidation in itself.'

'Yes,' said Mr Farmer. 'I am aware.' He leant forward across the desk. 'What names do they call you, Elizabeth? Something unkind?'

Her cheeks glowed. She couldn't bring herself to say what it was they called her.

'They've been calling her a snob,' said Mrs Muir. 'Just because she's come from a different sort of school . . . it's not been easy for her.'

'I'm sure it hasn't,' said Mr Farmer. 'It never is easy, moving from one environment to another. But the thing is, Elizabeth, that one has to learn to adjust. Fit in with new ways. The school you went to before was only for the few lucky people who could afford it. Here we cater for everybody. We have all sorts . . . clever ones, not so clever ones . . . rich ones, poor ones . . . black ones, white ones . . . we don't care whether people can afford it or not. To us, that's not important. What's important is what sort of person you are – not where you come from or how much money your parents have got. As far as we're concerned, you could live in a mud hut or a mansion; it wouldn't make the slightest scrap of difference, but only let people suspect for one moment that you're feeling superior, just because you've had advantages that they haven't, and I'm afraid it's only human nature that some of them are going to be a bit resentful.'

'I don't think she feels superior,' said Mrs Muir. 'I did tell her, before she came here, that just because she was probably going to find herself way ahead of everyone it didn't mean that she was necessarily any brighter than they were. I'm sure she doesn't think that. Do you?' She turned to Elizabeth for confirmation. 'It's just a question of – well! Of differences.'

'I see.' Mr Farmer also turned to Elizabeth. 'Do you feel yourself to be different, Elizabeth?'

'Not now,' said Elizabeth. 'I did at first. Just a little bit.'

'How about feeling superior?'

'I don't!'

How could she possibly feel superior to someone like Jo Ann, who was already in the over-14 netball team at the age of only eleven? Or Sammy English, who could make up jokes and keep people amused? Elizabeth couldn't make up a joke to save her life, and if she ever managed to get a place on the *class* netball team, never mind a *school* one, she would think herself lucky.

'Hm.' Mr Farmer was leaning back in his chair, pensively tapping a ruler against his fingertips. 'Tell me . . . have you made any friends since you've been here, Elizabeth? Any special friends.'

'She got on quite well with Sandra Gower,' said Mrs Muir. 'But unfortunately, of course, she left. Before that, it was the Dewar child.'

'Oh, yes?' Mr Farmer looked up, interested. 'What happened there?'

'Frankly, I discouraged it,' said Mrs Muir.

'Discouraged it? On what grounds?'

Just for a moment, Mrs Muir looked uncomfortable.

'Basically because I felt that she was a bad influence. I'll admit that I had also – been told things. About her background. I don't know whether I let that colour my judgement. I suppose subconsciously I may have done, but – well, it just didn't seem to me that it was a good idea.' Her voice tailed off. 'I don't know . . . I may, perhaps, have been wrong—'

'If I may say so, Mrs Muir—' even Elizabeth could detect the note of reproach in Mr Farmer's voice '—I think that you have. Children do just occasionally know what is best for themselves. In fact, rather more often, I sometimes suspect, than we give them credit for. Paddy Dewar would have been an excellent choice of friend! She's bright, she's alert, she's thoroughly likeable . . . she and Elizabeth could have done each other a world of good. Paddy has a great many qualities that Elizabeth could have benefited from. She could do with being taken out of herself – made a bit less serious. A bit less introspective. Even, perhaps, a bit more of a rebel? It certainly wouldn't have done her any harm.'

'No.' Mrs Muir sighed. 'You could be right. I confess I have wondered whether I ought just to have let things stand. Still—' she turned back, brightly, to Elizabeth '—it's not as if you've quarrelled or anything, is it? You could always ask Paddy if she'd like to come to tea again. This weekend, for example. How about this weekend? Why don't you try asking her?'

Because it was too late, thought Elizabeth. The damage had been done. She had hurt Paddy, and Paddy in return had hurt her. They could never be friends again now.

Mr Farmer was standing up.

'Let me take Elizabeth back to her classroom. I think that's probably the best thing we can do right now.'

Elizabeth looked up at him in horror. Even Mrs Muir seemed doubtful.

'Things will settle down,' said Mr Farmer. 'I promise you. They always do.' He held out a hand. 'Come on, Elizabeth! Let's go and see what they have to say for themselves . . . you're quite welcome to wait here, Mrs Muir, if you'd like, and we can discuss matters further when I get back, but I'm perfectly certain things will work out all right. Elizabeth's a sensible girl, and 1C aren't really such a bad lot – are they, Elizabeth?'

He smiled at her, hopefully. Elizabeth tried to smile back, but found that she couldn't; her lips had gone all trembly and wouldn't do anything but quiver.

'See how she feels about things this evening. After all, it is Friday . . . only a few more hours to go, then the whole weekend in front of you. Mm?' Mr Farmer tightened his grip on Elizabeth's hand. She wasn't sure whether it was meant to be comforting, or whether it was his way of telling her that she was going to go back and face 1C whether she liked it or not. 'So! What lessons do you have on a Friday afternoon? Anything nice?' Mr Farmer paused, in Miss George's office, to consult the master time-table. 'Aha! Double period of PE! Well, that can't be bad, can it?'

Elizabeth found her voice.

'But it's raining,' she said.

'Raining?' Mr Farmer sounded surprised. 'Is it? Why, so it is! Well, not to worry! Drop of rain never hurt anyone.'

'But it means we can't play netball,' said Elizabeth.

'Oh, she's netball mad!' said Mrs Muir. 'You'd think it was the only reason for coming to school . . . go on! Off with you.' She gave Elizabeth a little push. 'I'll see you later – and don't forget! Ask Paddy if she'd like to come to tea.'

Elizabeth was led away, down the corridor, her hand still firmly clasped in Mr Farmer's. The rain, by now, had set in with dismal constancy, dripping off the roof tops, dribbling down the windows.

'I'm afraid it rather looks as if it's here to stay, doesn't it?' said Mr Farmer. 'Still! All can't surely be lost? What happens instead of netball? You're never telling me they're mean enough to make you stay indoors and do sums!'

'No.' Elizabeth spoke glumly. She would almost have preferred sums. 'We have to go into the hall and run races.'

'So what's wrong with running races? I should have thought you'd be quite good at it – you look as though you should be. You've got nice long legs. At any rate, it must be better than doing fractions? Mm?' Mr Farmer winked at her. 'Can't say I care for fractions all that much myself . . .'

1C were in the middle of Improvisation with Miss Crompton. All the desks had been arranged in two long rows to represent market stalls – she remembered that they had been going to do a street market scene, with people buying and selling. As the door opened, they heard Redmond's voice: ''Matoes! Luvly ripe 'matoes!' and Paddy's, in competition: 'Cockles 'n whelks! Cockles 'n whelks!' Sammy English was dancing up and down on his desk lid, Michael Armstrong pushing an imaginary barrow. There was Julie Christmas, trying on clothes, Jo Ann clipping an unseen infant round the ear . . . They weren't at all happy at being interrupted; Elizabeth could see that they weren't. She didn't blame them. She wouldn't have been happy had she been taking part. She could feel them all staring at her, accusingly.

'Miss Crompton—' Mr Farmer stood, holding the door. 'I do apologize for butting in on you like this, but something rather important. If I might just talk to the class for a few moments?'

Miss Crompton, in a fluster, said: 'Of course, Mr Farmer. Would you like me to leave?'

'Well, perhaps if you wouldn't mind.' (Elizabeth could almost hear the silent groans.) 'I wouldn't normally ask it of you, but—'

'No, no! That's quite all right. We'd practically finished.' Miss Crompton gathered up her papers and stuffed them higgledy-piggledy into her brief case. 'Just so long as they remember to put the desks back.'

'They can do that straight away,' said Mr Farmer. 'In fact, I should like to see you all sitting in your accustomed places – and as quickly as possible, please.' He nodded at Redmond, who happened to be the nearest. 'Go on, then! Jump to it!'

1C jumped. They might not have been too happy about it, but not even Redmond dared argue with Mr Farmer. Elizabeth stood at the front, feeling like a traitor – like someone who had gone running home to tell tales and get people into trouble.

'Right, then,' said Mr Farmer. 'If everybody is settled—'

Fat had reappeared. She was sitting at her desk

162

with her eyes fixed firmly on Mr Farmer, not looking at Elizabeth. Paddy wasn't looking at Elizabeth, either. Nor was she looking at Mr Farmer: she was busy pulling her fringe down over her eyes, trying to make it reach as far as the top of her nose. Elizabeth saw that her cut finger had been covered in a strip of sticking plaster.

'*If* everybody is settled,' said Mr Farmer. Julie Christmas sat up, brightly. Jo Ann scowled. 'I have a very serious matter that I wish to raise with you . . . at some time during the dinner break this morning a paperweight belonging to Elizabeth was either deliberately or accidentally smashed. Is there anyone who can tell me anything about it?'

There was a long silence. Elizabeth didn't dare to look at Paddy. She looked at Fat, instead, expecting at least an indication of 'I told you so' to appear on her face – for in fairness, Fat *had* told her – but Fat had her head bent and seemed to be studying something on her desk lid.

'Well?' said Mr Farmer. 'I'm waiting . . . *yes*, Paddy? You have something to say?'

Elizabeth's stomach turned upside down. For a moment she felt almost as if she were going to be sick. She heard Paddy's voice, small and rather tremulous.

'Please, sir, I found it.'

'How do you mean, you found it.'

'When I came back to the classroom. During dinner hour.' Slowly, Elizabeth raised her eyes. Paddy was looking at her, across the room. She seemed to be speaking directly to Elizabeth rather than Mr Farmer. 'It was there, on the floor . . . all smashed up. I tried to put it together again, but there were too many pieces. So I just picked up the little figures and put them in your desk – put them in Elizabeth's desk.'

It was as if a lead weight had been lifted. A great surge of pure joy went flooding through Elizabeth. It hadn't been Paddy! It hadn't been Paddy after all! She should have known that it wasn't. She should have *known* that Paddy would never be capable of playing such a mean trick.

Mr Farmer was frowning; he seemed still to have doubts.

'You say that you came back to the classroom during the dinner break – I need hardly tell you that that is strictly against school rules. What exactly did you come back here for?'

Beneath her freckles, Paddy turned rather pink.

'I came to look at it.'

'I beg your pardon?'

'I c-came to l-look at it.'

'Look at it? Look at what? Look at the *paperweight*?' Paddy nodded. Her cheeks, by now, were bright scarlet. Elizabeth wished that Mr Farmer would stop asking her questions. She hated to see Paddy made embarrassed. 'You mean,' said Mr Farmer, 'that you were deliberately going to go to another girl's desk and take out something that didn't belong to you?'

There was a silence. Paddy looked miserable.

'If you wanted to look at the paperweight,' said Mr Farmer, 'why did you not ask Elizabeth?'

'Don't know.'

'Did you think she wouldn't let you?'

Paddy pulled at her fringe.

'Don't know.'

'Surely you usually ask people before helping yourself to their possessions? You wouldn't normally take something that didn't belong to you?'

Paddy twisted a strand of fringe round one finger.

'S'pose not.'

'Well, then!'

Mr Farmer was plainly expecting some kind of an explanation. Elizabeth knew that Paddy didn't have one; not without giving away the fact that they had quarrelled.

'Actually,' she said, 'it did *sort* of belong to her . . . it sort of belonged to both of us.'

Mr Farmer switched his gaze.

'Now, what,' he said, mildly, 'is that supposed to mean? "Sort of"?'

'We sort of . . . shared it,' said Elizabeth.

'Oh! So you sort of shared it, did you?'

'They did,' said Jo Ann. 'They shared it.'

'Yeah, that's right, they did, 'cos *she*—' Redmond jerked his thumb disparagingly towards Paddy '—tried to tell me I 'ad to wash me bleedin' 'ands before I could bleedin' well touch it.'

'I see.' Mr Farmer swung back again to Paddy. 'Very well, then, so you shared the paperweight, and Elizabeth didn't mind you going to her desk. However, that still leaves us with the original question of who was responsible for the damage.'

Elizabeth felt that she didn't care any more who was responsible. Now that she knew it wasn't Paddy, it no longer seemed to matter.

'Who else,' said Mr Farmer, 'came back to the classroom during the dinner break? Anyone?'

No one, apparently. But suddenly Elizabeth looked at Fat's bent head, and she knew. From the simple fact that everyone else was looking up – looking round – craning to see if any guilty hands were being raised – she *knew*. Fat was the only one who wasn't looking up. *Because Fat was the one who had done it.*

'We shall have to assume,' said Mr Farmer, after waiting a suitable length of time, 'that it was someone, therefore, from another class. We have also to assume that it was a genuine accident. I cannot bring myself to believe that any pupil in this school would be petty enough, or spiteful enough, to perpetrate such a deed out of sheer malice.'

Fat's head bent even lower. I shall never speak to her again, thought Elizabeth. Never, as long as I live.

The bell rang for the end of the period. Outside, the rain was still slashing.

'All right,' said Mr Farmer. 'Hold your horses – just sit down again, Redmond. You can go when I've finished with you and not before. There's a bit of re-arranging I want to do first . . . you!' He pointed a finger at Paddy. 'I don't like you sitting there, at the extreme back of the class. As I recall, every single report you've ever had since coming to this school has included the words "talks too much". No girl who talks too much should ever be allowed to hide herself away at the back. You come down here and change with someone – Jo Ann. It wouldn't hurt you to take a back seat for once. Elizabeth, where do you sit?' Shyly, Elizabeth pointed to her empty desk in the middle of the room. 'Well, that's no place for a new girl is it? New girls should always be kept down at the front, until it's been discovered whether they're going to be talkers or concentrators. Dawn, you're a concentrator. You go and take Elizabeth's seat. Elizabeth, you sit down at the front with Paddy. Redmond, if you don't keep still I shall be forced to the conclusion that you have St Vitus' Dance. All right, you girls, that'll do for now. You can sort out the details later. But first thing Monday morning, I want everyone in her alloted place – and I shall personally come round to check, so be warned. Redmond, you may now move. Elizabeth, a word with you.'

Redmond went off at a gallop, closely followed by the rest of the class. One or two – Sammy English, Jo Ann, Janet Newman – paused just long enough to give Elizabeth rather sheepish grins. Paddy, still red-faced beneath her freckles, didn't look at her; neither did Fat.

'Now, then.' Mr Farmer waited until the last person had gone stampeding out of the room. 'What are we going to do about this paperweight? Are you still convinced that it was broken on purpose?'

Now that she stopped to think about it, she wasn't quite so certain. She knew *who* had broken it – but had she really done it on purpose? Or had it just slipped through her fingers by mistake? Everyone knew that Fat was clumsy. She couldn't help it. She was just all fingers and thumbs. 'Would you like me to read out a notice about it in assembly, asking the culprit to own up?'

Elizabeth hesitated.

'I don't guarantee it will produce any results,' said Mr Farmer, 'but it might give him or her a few uneasy moments.'

Fat certainly deserved some uneasy moments; not a doubt about that.

'Well?' said Mr Farmer. 'What do you think?'

'I think, perhaps, that we ought not to bother,' said Elizabeth. 'I don't really mind all that much . . . not really.'

Down in the cloakroom, she found that she was alone; all the others had already changed and gone back up to the hall. For a moment she was almost tempted to stay where she was. Almost certainly no one would miss her, and Miss Woods practically never took a register. But then, to stay away from classes was against the rules, and Elizabeth had been brought up to believe that rules were there for a purpose. You didn't question them, and you didn't break them; you just obeyed them, because that was what they were there for. Suddenly it struck her: could that be what Mr Farmer had meant by his strange remark about how it would do her good to become a bit more of a rebel? Surely he didn't mean that she *ought* to break the rules? Even as she stood pondering the idea, the second bell rang; it was enough to galvanize her into action. You just didn't do things like deliberately staying away from class.

Nonetheless, as she reached the hall her heart sank. She had been hoping against hope that maybe *this* time, *this* Friday, it might not be races but something different – games with bean bags or even just boring exercises – but she could see that Miss Woods had already appointed the four team leaders. The boys were Sammy English and Michael Armstrong, the girls were Julie Christmas and Paddy. They had obviously had just the one round of picking up. Sammy English had chosen Jo Ann, and Michael had chosen Janet Newman; Julie had John Diamond, and Paddy had Redmond. Elizabeth slunk across the hall and secreted herself behind Carmen and a couple of others. Perhaps if she could manage to stay hidden right till the end, Miss Woods would think that that was why she hadn't been chosen, because nobody had known that she was there.

She heard Sammy English choosing a boy called Kevin Marshall, who was good at hop-skip-and-jumping. She heard Julie Christmas choose Dawn Forrest, and Michael Armstrong pick a weedy boy called Simon Jestico, who couldn't run for toffee but happened to be his best friend. Then there was a long pause, and Miss Woods said: 'Paddy?'

'I'll have—' Agonizing wait while Paddy decided who she would have. 'I'll have Elizabeth,' said Paddy.

'Elizabeth?' Miss Woods sounded doubtful. 'I don't think I've seen Elizabeth. Is she—'

'Yes!' Elizabeth bounded out from behind her protective covering. The heart which a moment ago had been sinking like a sack of cement now joyously soared as if it had wings. 'I'm here!'

'Oh, so you decided to return to us?' said Miss Woods.'

Caught in mid-bound, Elizabeth suddenly remembered. Her heart, abruptly shedding its wings, came crashing back to earth.

'I'm very sorry,' she said, 'about not stopping when you called me.'

'I forgive you,' said Miss Woods. 'Just this once

. . . do I take it that everything has now been brought to a satisfactory conclusion?'

Elizabeth beamed.

'Yes, *thank* you,' she said.

'Good! Off you go, then. Sammy! Your turn.'

As Elizabeth settled into place behind Redmond, Paddy squirming to see round him, whispered: 'I *didn't* do it . . . *honestly.*'

Elizabeth whispered back: 'I know you didn't.'

'But did you think that I did?'

'Only just for a moment.'

'I knew you would.'

'It was only just at first. When I first saw it.'

'But you still thought it.'

'I didn't! Truly! Not deep down.'

'Shuddup bloody yacking,' said Redmond. He poked a finger in Paddy's ribs. 'It's your turn. Pick Abdul. He's the best one left.'

Paddy, obediently, picked Abdul. She craned back again to Elizabeth.

'What are you going to tell your mother?'

'I've already told her.'

'Is she mad?'

'Not really. She just said I shouldn't have brought it here . . . she wants to know if you'd like to come to tea on Saturday.'

'*Saturday?*'

'Yes.'

'*This* Saturday?'

'Yes.'

'You mean *tomorrow*?'

'*Yes.*' That was Redmond, growing impatient. 'She just said so, didn't she? What's the matter with you? You going deaf, or something?'

170

Paddy took no notice of Redmond.

'I'll bring a present with me . . . what shall I bring? Does she like chocolates? Or would she prefer flowers?'

'Flowers, I think, but you don't have to. She won't—'

'But I want to! I've got all this money – I'm doing a paper round. I'm earning five pounds a week. It—'

'Bleedin' 'ell!' said Redmond. 'Can't you give your bleedin' arse a chance?'

Elizabeth giggled. Paddy said: 'Don't swear. People only use swear words when they can't think of anything else.'

'Get lost,' said Redmond, unimpressed. 'It's your turn again.'

'Oh!' Paddy spun round. 'Who shall we pick?'

There wasn't much of a selection left. They were down to the odds and ends – down to the unfortunates whom nobody wanted. Last week, thought Elizabeth, she had been among those unfortunates. Fat was among them still. She saw her standing there, looking, if such a thing were possible, even larger and more lumpish in T-shirt and shorts than in a skirt and blouse.

'Shall we have Maureen?' said Paddy. 'She's not too bad.'

To her surprise, Elizabeth heard her own voice saying: 'Don't have Maureen . . . have Fat.'

'*Fat?*'

'Are you crazy?' Redmond looked at her, indignantly. 'She's no bleedin' use.'

'It's not her fault,' said Elizabeth. 'She can't help it.'

172

'Course she bleedin' can!'

'No, she can't.'

'Yes, she bleedin' well—'

'Paddy!' Miss Woods's voice rang out, across the hall. 'Hurry up! It's your go.'

'We'll have Fat,' said Paddy.

'Bleedin' 'ell!' Redmond turned away in disgust.

'I do *wish* you would stop swearing,' said Paddy. 'You don't hear Elizabeth and me doing it, do you?'

Redmond's lip curled.

'Oh, you're just bleedin' perfect,' he said, 'you two . . .'

BLACK BEAUTY'S FAMILY 1

Diana and Christine Pullein-Thompson

Here are two stories about Black Beauty's relations. Black Romany, three generations before Black Beauty, was a well-bred horse who lived at Belvoir Castle. He hunted with Prince Albert and had lots of exciting adventures trekking across England. Blossom, six generations later, was not so lucky. The product of an unfortunate alliance, she had a life of drudgery working as a cart-horse, and her future seemed bleak until, out of the blue, came unexpected success.

If you're an eager Beaver reader, perhaps you ought to try some more of our exciting titles. They are available in bookshops or they can be ordered directly from us. Just complete the form below and enclose the right amount of money and the books will be sent to you.

And if you would like to hear more about Beaver Books, and find out all the latest news, don't forget the Beaver Bulletin. If you just send a stamped, self-addressed envelope to Beaver Books, 17-21 Conway Street, London W1P 6JD and we will send you one.

If you would like to order books, please send this form with the money due to:

HAMLYN PAPERBACK CASH SALES, PO BOX 11, FALMOUTH, CORNWALL TR10 9EN.

Send a cheque or postal order, and don't forget to include postage at the following rates: UK: 55p for the first book, 22p for the second, 14p for each additional book; BFPO and Eire: 55p for the first book, 22p for the second, 14p for the next seven books and 8p per book thereafter. Overseas: £1.00 for first book and 25p for each additional book.

NAME...

ADDRESS..

....

Please print clearly